A noi

Stuart David is a musician, songwriter and novelist. He grew up in Alexandria, on the west coast of Scotland – a town memorably described as looking like 'a town that's helping the police with their inquiries'. Stuart co-founded the band Belle and Sebastian (1996–2000) and went on to form Looper in 1998. His memoir, *In the All-Night Café: A Memoir of Belle and Sebastian's Formative Year*, was published by Abacus/Little, Brown in 2015 to much critical acclaim.

Peacock's Alibi

STUART DAVID

Polygon

First published in Great Britain in 2018 by Polygon, an imprint of
Birlinn Ltd.

Birlinn Ltd
West Newington House
10 Newington Road
Edinburgh
EH9 1QS

www.polygonbooks.co.uk

1

ISBN 978 1 84697 411 3
eBook ISBN 978 0 85790 987 9

British Library Cataloguing-in-Publication Data
A catalogue record for this book is available on request
from the British Library.

Typeset by 3btype.com, Edinburgh
Printed and bound by Clays Ltd, St Ives plc

Peacock's Alibi

Most days, I wouldn't be over the moon to find a detective inspector standing on my doorstep – especially one who'd come round to drill down into the finer points of my whereabouts on the night Dougie Dowds was murdered. But this afternoon, when my old pal Detective Inspector McFadgen turned up at the front door with that specific aim in mind, it came as something of a welcome relief. It got me away from the bedlam that was playing itself out in the living room, the pandemonium that had peaked about half an hour earlier, and stayed right up there, with no obvious signs of abating. And for that much, at least, I was eternally grateful to the boy McFadgen.

Here's what had been going down . . .

The wife had a full-length mirror propped up against the back of the couch, and she was standing looking into it – in tears – all trussed up in the elaborate pink bridesmaid's dress she was meant to wear at her daft pal's upcoming wedding.

'I look like a meringue,' the wife moaned. 'Look at me. Wilma must have lost her mind. How can she possibly be expecting me to go out in public wearing this?'

Meanwhile, the wife's mother was sitting across the room in an armchair – but rather than offering any of the emotional support you might expect under the circumstances, she was using the subject of the upcoming wedding to put forward her own agenda, an agenda that was never very far from the forefront of her concerns, no matter what other events might be going on round about her.

'Wasn't Wilma married once already?' she said, and the wife nodded silently, the wee shoulders moving up and down as she sobbed away to herself. 'Well, there you go,' the mother said. 'It's just like I'm always telling you, Beverley – marriage doesn't have to be for life nowadays. Just make sure you try and catch the bouquet at this wedding, and let fate take care of the rest. You could be shot of this idiot here by the end of the year. Who knows, you might even meet a nice young man at the wedding itself. It was at a wedding Marianne met her husband.'

I shot the mother-in-law a look, but she stared straight back at me, totally nonplussed.

'This is probably the sort of stuff you're meant to keep for behind my back, Mrs Cuthbertson,' I said. 'An air of frosty disapproval in my company would be enough to get your point across.'

'Oh Jesus Christ!' the wife shouted. She'd turned round

so's her back was facing the mirror and she was staring at her reflection now by looking over her shoulder. 'Look at the size of my arse in this thing, Peacock,' she said. 'Look at it! It's tiny. It's all squashed flat. She *must* have done that deliberately. Can you see it? *Look* at it!'

'That Eric Smiley was asking after you again, Beverley,' the mother said. 'Do you remember Eric? He's got a lovely house now. Still a bachelor too. I've always thought Eric had a really lovely head of hair on him.'

'It's so's none of us outshine her,' Bev said. 'She's *trying* to make us look like houfers. Come and look at my arse from here, Peacock. Does it really look as wee as it does in the mirror? Be honest with me. It does, doesn't it? It must. She's at it, isn't she? Oh my God! What am I going to *do*, Peacock?'

She flung herself at me then, throwing her arms over my shoulders and enveloping me in the acres of pink silk and pink netting. Hysterics, I suppose you'd call it – the wailing, the difficulty breathing, the clawing at me. I was just about at the end of my tether, partly owing to the fact that the mother-in-law still didn't show any signs of letting up on the new-man front. But thankfully, that was the exact moment Detective Inspector McFadgen decided to launch his assault on the front door.

'Answer that, Mum,' the wife said in a muffled voice, and the mother pushed and tutted her way past us, struggling to get through the tangle of limbs and bridesmaid's dress that were blocking her way.

I'll tell you this, though, she was fair glad she'd made the effort when she found out who it was that had interrupted our scene of cosy domesticity.

'Peacock!' she shouted, making sure as many of the neighbours as possible could hear her. 'It's for you. It's the police. Homicide!'

And as I untangled myself from the wife's embrace, the mother-in-law practically skipped back into the room, about as happy as I'd seen her in the past ten years, and she said to the wife, 'You're free, Beverley. They've got him at last. It's been a long time coming, but he's finally about to get his comeuppance.'

'For God's sake, Mum,' the wife said, 'I'm at the end of my rope here. Be serious for once. Look at this dress. Look at it!'

And I slipped quietly out into the hallway, and told Detective Inspector McFadgen to come away in, to follow me into the kitchen. And if there hadn't already been the kind of history between us that tends to keep things on a somewhat formal footing, I'd probably have grabbed his hand and given it a right good shaking, or maybe even pulled him in for a quick bear hug.

We go way back, the bold detective and myself. Back, in fact, to when he was simply PC McFadgen, at least. Here's the thing about him, though – regardless of the rank he happens to be occupying at any particular moment, he's always trying to lift me for a crime at the level he's currently qualified to be investigating. He apparently sees us as rising up through the ranks of our respective careers almost in parallel. I mean, fair enough, he's booked me for this and that, now and again. But the vast bulk of it was minor misdemeanours back in the early days. He's been pretty much on to plums since then. Still, give him his due, he's a determined soul. Not a man prone to giving up when he sets his mind to something.

Worse luck.

'What can I get you, Duncan?' I asked him, when I'd ushered him through the lobby and into the kitchen. 'Tea, coffee? A wee snifter?'

'Nothing for me, Johnson,' he said. 'This is hardly a social call.'

'Fair enough,' I said, and grabbed myself a beer from the fridge. 'Settle yourself down at the table there, and let's hear the latest. Let's see what I've been up to this time.'

He started ruffling about in his jacket pockets, first the ones on the inside, then he found what he was looking for in one at the front.

Now that McFadgen's out of the uniform, and free to put his own distinct wardrobe together, it's hard to pin-point exactly what kind of look he's going for. He's certainly attempting something or other, but he's fallen somewhat short of whatever it was, and he really just looks like a bit of a fud. There's certainly a stab at Humphrey Bogart in there, maybe some Taggart and even a hint of Columbo. But his lumpy wee body, his pink face and his flat brown hair have resulted in the whole thing making him look more like the treasurer of a bowling club than whatever it was he initially set out to achieve. Unless, of course, it was the treasurer of a bowling club he was aiming at all along.

'Right,' he said, now that he'd laid his hands on the precious item that had been hiding away in his suit pocket, 'what have you got to say about this, Johnson? What fabricated nonsense am I going to have to sit and listen to in response to this?'

And he handed me a resealable plastic bag about the size of a fag packet, with what appeared to be a single piece of paper inside it. A blank piece of paper, as far as I could tell.

I held the bag up in front of me and gave it a right good staring at, more just to humour the guy than anything else, and after a few seconds he started drumming his fingers on the tabletop and nodding at me slowly.

'That'll do, eh?' he said. 'I suppose even a patter merchant like you knows when to call it a day.'

I lifted my eyes from what I imagined must be Exhibit A and fixed them on him instead.

'That's the miracle that's going to get you off my streets once and for all,' he said. 'This city'll be a much cleaner place with you inside, and that item right there will put you inside for longer than you can possibly imagine.'

I started to wonder if the poor guy was maybe just a

touch overworked. Declining police numbers and all that malarkey – the constantly increasing paperwork. Maybe it had finally got to him. Or maybe he'd just never been all that stable in the first place.

'What exactly am I looking at here, Duncan?' I said. 'All I can see is a blank bit of paper. I think I must be missing its wider significance. What exactly is it?'

The pink face grew pinker. He reached out with a speed that suggested we were about to witness an instance of police brutality. But it was the plastic bag he grabbed – pulled the thing out of my hands, took a quick swatch at it and then turned it round and handed it back to me. Suddenly things were slightly clearer. It wasn't a blank bit of paper at all – there were some words printed on it, and numbers. Closer inspection revealed it, in fact, to be a receipt of some sort. We were starting to get somewhere. I was still none the wiser as to how this innocuous item was the weapon that could relieve the Glasgow streets of my looming presence, but at least we'd established that there must be some method to McFadgen's madness, rather than just the beginnings of a full-scale mental collapse.

'Are you recognising it now?' he said, but I had to come clean and tell him I wasn't.

'I can see it's a receipt, Duncan,' I said, 'but that's as far as it goes. What's the story behind it?'

'Take a closer look,' he said. 'Take a look at the items on it. Read them out. See if they ring any bells.'

There were only three. A bottle of Irn-Bru, a packet of chewing gum and a magazine, which from its title seemed to be of a distinctly pornographic nature. Still, I read the list out to keep the good detective happy, and he raised his eyebrows and tipped his head at an angle that suggested he'd just given me an insight into the fundamental workings of the universe.

'Bingo!' he said. 'I take it you recognise that collection of junk, Johnson.'

I thought about it for a minute and then I told him I still seemed to be somewhat wide of the mark.

'Look at the credit card number at the top of the receipt,' he said. 'Look familiar?'

The number was interrupted by four Xs in the middle, four digits at the start, four at the end.

'Should it seem familiar?' I asked him.

'It certainly should.'

'How come?'

He gave me the head tip again. ''Cause it's yours.'

I wasn't about to start arguing with him. It might very well have been mine – it's hardly the sort of thing you commit to memory, is it? So I gave him the benefit of the doubt and I looked over the list of items again.

'So what are we saying here?' I asked him.

'We're saying I've got you bang to rights, Johnson. At last. It's all over. You're done.'

'For buying a porno mag? Have you gone mental,

Duncan? That's what all this has been about? You've burst in here, threatening me with this, that and the next thing – telling me you've got what you need to fulfil your mad desire to lock me up and throw away the key – and this is what the whole scenario amounts to? I bought a porno mag? You've been overdoing it, Duncan. Seriously. You need a good long holiday, pal. A few quiet weeks in the south of France. Besides which, since when did it even become an offence to buy a porn mag?'

He gave me an evil wee smile, and then slapped at the plastic bag as it hung loosely in my grip.

'It's got nothing to do with what you actually *bought*,' he said. 'Your perverted desires are your own affair. All that matters to me is *when* you bought that filth, Peacock. Have a look at the date. Have a look at the time.'

If I have to be honest, the whole thing was starting to wear a bit thin by this point. It had been a novelty to get out of the madness that was taking place in the living room for a while, but the madness that had replaced it was starting to seem like the decidedly less appealing of the two options. And given the choice now I decided I'd rather be back in there with the wife banging on about the size of her arse than take much more of McFadgen's receipt mania. I quickly checked the date and time he was talking about, read them out, and did what I could to hurry this thing along and send him on his own sweet way again.

'The twenty-third of June,' he said. 'Ten minutes past

eight in the evening. That was Thursday night, Peacock. Thursday. And according to you . . . let me just get this right . . .'

Back he went into the jacket pockets again, first one then the other. Then back to the first one. Eventually he produced a notebook and opened it up on the table. Flicking through the pages and licking the tip of his finger here and there till he found what he was looking for.

'There it is,' he said, 'right there. According to you, at eight ten on Thursday night, you were sitting in Rogano's with your wife, splashing out on an expensive dinner for your anniversary. You've got the waiter backing up your story. You've got various other customers backing up your story. You've got your wife backing up your story. And yet, there it is, in black and white. This receipt is telling another story altogether, Johnson. This receipt is saying that at that exact time you were a good couple of miles away from Rogano's, in Barrett's on Byres Road, buying a wank mag and a tin of Irn-Bru. And that, as you well know, puts you right in the frame for whacking Dougie Dowds. That Rogano's alibi was all that was standing between you and a life sentence, Peacock. And now that alibi is out the window. Kaput, my friend. And that makes this just about the happiest day of my short, sweet life.'

2

Dougie Dowds was a notorious grass. Whenever he found himself in hot water with McFadgen's crew, which was frequently, he'd invariably have a juicy titbit on somebody else that he'd be willing to trade for his own freedom. But more than that, he'd regularly take a tip-off to McFadgen even when he was in the clear, in return for a wad of cash. And normally that kind of behaviour would get you seen to quick smart – the concrete wellies, the sharp blow to the back of the head. Whatever.

Here's the thing about Dougie, though, here's the twist in the tale: just about everybody, up to and including the myriad of mugs he'd grassed on over the years – even the ones who'd spent time behind bars due to his transactions with McFadgen – felt somehow protective towards him.

You could hardly help yourself.

He was such a fucked-up and bewildered-seeming wee guy that it was like trying to deal with a cat you'd just fished out the river. And he never made any secret of what he was up to with McFadgen and his boys.

'I'm a right rotten bastard,' he'd tell you. Or 'I can hardly look you in the eye, Peacock. I'm eating myself up here.' And somehow you'd end up trying to reassure him that he was all right. Which he was. He was a sweetheart when it came right down to it. He'd a heart of gold. Apart from the selling every bastard to the filth, that is. And before you knew it you'd probably have lent him a bit of money into the bargain, or bought him a bag of groceries – and there he'd go on his merry way, still eating himself up with guilt about whoever it was he'd just landed in the shite this time.

So there you are – that was Dougie Dowds. That's how he was. Until the evening of the twenty-third of June – some time after eight o'clock – when McFadgen's minions found him lying on the concrete pad beside the bins, two floors beneath his balcony, having left nothing much up there as evidence bar the signs of a rather brutal struggle.

Poor wee bastard.

'When I came round here to see you the day before yesterday,' McFadgen said, all fired up with excitement now, 'I knew it was you that killed Dougie. I'd come round here to arrest you. Then, when you hit me with that pile of mince you're calling an alibi, I'd no option but to go away again and work on blowing the thing to smithereens.

And this receipt does exactly that, Johnson. *Exactly* that. So, what are you saying to it?'

I took a minute to consider what I *was* saying to it.

'How about I ask you a question?' was what I came up with in the end. 'Will you answer me a question, Duncan?'

He looked at me in exasperation, no doubt just itching to get the cuffs on me and start battering on about my right to remain silent. But he kept himself under control, took the plastic bag with the receipt in it out of my hands, and tucked it away safely in his inside pocket.

'Get on with it, then,' he told me. 'Whatever nonsense you're trying to pull won't wash, Peacock. I've got you fair and square. But ask me your pish and then let's get going.'

'Fair enough,' I said. 'It's nothing fancy, Duncan. Just answer me this. One simple thing: are you a reader of the books of Ian Rankin by any chance?'

He frowned at me.

'What the hell's that got to do with anything?' he said. 'Is this a wind-up?'

'Never mind,' I said. 'Just answer the question. Do you read them?'

'Aye,' he said. 'I read them.'

'Right. And you've read that one he put *me* in? *A Question of Blood*?'

'I've read them all. Cover to cover.'

'Right. So when did you first read the one he put me in? When did you get round to that one?'

13

He hummed and hawed for a bit. It's always the same when you ask a member of the constabulary about the boy Rankin – all other thoughts head north, and they're totally lost in their fanboy obsessions.

Try it some time.

Never fails.

'It must be about a year and a half ago,' he said. 'I don't read them in order. I think I read that one in Spain with Liz. Just after Christmas. The Christmas before last.'

'I knew you must have read it,' I told him.

He seemed to snap out of it then, a tad embarrassed he'd taken his eye off the ball, and the face flushed pink as his blood got up.

'What the hell are you talking about?' he said. 'What's this got to do with anything? What's it got to do with the fact that you're the murdering bastard that killed wee Dougie Dowds?'

'It's got plenty to do with the fact that you *think* I killed Dougie Dowds,' I said. 'Plenty. Look at it this way, McFadgen. We've never been the best of pals. Fair enough. But up until you read that book, you knew the kind of thing I got into. You were clear-sighted enough about where I drew the line, and how far I'd go beyond it at a push. But for about a year and a half now you've been hounding me about shite you'd never have thought twice about connecting me to in the past.'

'Bollocks!'

'Bollocks it's bollocks. It's that book to blame, McFadgen. The book's a fiction. The Rankin boy blew me up out of all proportion – took a few rumours he'd heard here and there and exaggerated me beyond belief. That's their job, Duncan. Writers, they write fiction. But a wheen of folk've been treating me differently ever since they read that book, you included. I've been smeared. Look at last month, when you were hounding me non-stop about that stolen painting. You're developing an unhealthy obsession with me, McFadgen. It's getting to the stage where I'm starting to wonder if I should be having a quiet word with your superiors.'

'Johnson,' he said, closing his notebook and putting it back in the pocket it had come from, 'you're a bullshit merchant – always have been, always will be. You know you stole that painting from Pollok House. I know you stole that painting from Pollok House. And you know that I know that you stole it. You also know Dougie Dowds was about to hook me up with the final bit of evidence I needed to prove it, and that's how come he ended up lying on the concrete two floors beneath his veranda.'

'You're living in a fantasy land, Duncan,' I said. 'How could I possibly have got that painting out of Pollok House?'

'You're the only person who *could* have got it out of there,' McFadgen said. 'And on Thursday morning Dougie Dowds phoned me to arrange a meet-up to fill me in on just how you managed it. For a fee. But you found out about that, and you got to him before I could, and this receipt in my pocket proves that cause it puts you within a five-minute walk of his flat five minutes after he was killed. Miles away from where you claim you were at the time. Add to that the fact that his living room was liberally sprinkled with your fingerprints, and that there were even traces of your DNA on the jacket he was wearing, and I don't see how you can stand there in front of me spouting the pish you're spouting with a straight face.'

I took a good hit at my beer.

'Here's how,' I told him. 'For a start, Dougie was a pal – of course my fingerprints were in his living room. And what the fuck would I be doing buying a packet of chewing gum and a porno mag five minutes after I'd whacked a guy? Is that normal behaviour? "Okay, deed done, Peacock. What you really need now to calm yourself down is a right good chew and a quick wank." Are you mental, McFadgen?'

There was a brief interlude at this point. Before the detective inspector could expound any further on his theories, the kitchen door burst open and we were suddenly treated to an explosion of pink chiffon as the wife came stoating into the room, still worked all the way up to high doh.

'I thought you must still be here, Duncan,' she said. 'I think I need your opinion on something. Have you got a minute?'

McFadgen, God bless him, managed to disguise his initial reaction to her costume before she'd quite had time to clock it. But it was still somewhat obvious that he was badly shaken by the vision that had appeared before him.

'Tell me what you think of this dress, Duncan,' she said. 'Your honest opinion, mind, no holding back. How does this look to you?'

'Eh . . .' he stammered.

'It's bloody awful, isn't it?' the wife demanded, and I saw the relief in McFadgen's face. He'd been fully engaged in trying to find something positive to say about the thing, and it was perfectly obvious he'd been coming up with absolutely nothing.

'This is what Wilma Caldwell wants me to wear to her wedding. I'm a bridesmaid. I'd been looking forward to it too. I've never been a bridesmaid before – maybe once, when I was a wee girl, at my Aunt Carol's wedding, but I don't even remember that. This is my first time as an adult. Somebody told me you're not supposed to be a bridesmaid if you're already married. Do you know if that's right, Duncan?'

'It might be,' he said. 'I don't think there's a law against it, though.'

The wife laughed a bit too much at his lame witticism, and then carried on with her monologue.

'I don't know what to do,' she said. 'I said to Peacock earlier that I think Wilma's *trying* to make me look bad, so's I don't take any of the attention away from her. Not that I'd even want to. It's her big day. But how can I even go out in *public* in a thing like this?'

She stopped for breath and turned her back on McFadgen, turning her head to look at him over her shoulder. 'Look at my bum,' she said. 'Look at it. Can you even see it? All this material here. What's that even for? Have you ever seen anything like that in your puff? It makes me look totally arseless. And look at these sleeves. What's going on there? Is the whole thing as bad as I think it is, Duncan? Tell me the truth.'

McFadgen looked to me for help, but I was hardly likely to bail him out on this one, given the current state of our relationship. He was on his own as far as I was concerned. And I have to hand it to the guy, given the delicacy of the situation, he manoeuvred himself out of the danger zone quite admirably.

'Put it this way, Beverley,' he said in the end, 'at least at the wedding your husband won't be sticking out like a sore thumb, embarrassing you with the tackiness of his outfit.'

He was fair taking a liberty – considering I was sitting there in my best vintage Hawaiian shirt and a pair of Versace jeans. But his kowtowing to the wife cheered her up considerably, and the fact that somebody was putting the boot into yours truly had something of a knock-on effect. Like a shark smelling blood, the mother-in-law was suddenly on the scene, deeply impressed as always by anyone who's in the business of sullying my good name. That's pretty much all it takes to win her over to your cause.

'Let me ask you a question,' she said as she struggled past Bev's dress to get into the room and into the detective's line of sight. 'Are you single?'

The wife took a deep breath. 'That's my mum,' she said to McFadgen. 'Mrs Cuthbertson.'

'Pleased to meet you, Mrs Cuthbertson,' McFadgen said, but the mother wasn't in the mood for formalities.

'Call me Mary,' she said, 'and answer my question. Are you single?'

McFadgen shook his head. 'I've been happily married for fifteen years,' he said, well aware that he'd totally lost control of the situation for now, and that all he could do was wait and see how things panned out.

'That's a pity,' the mother-in-law said, 'a real pity. I'm disappointed to hear that, Duncan. I really am. You're exactly the kind of man Beverley should be looking for, in my opinion. I keep telling her – kick that idiot to the kerb. Am I right? You're still a good looking girl, I tell her. That won't always be the case. Find yourself something better before you start going to seed. But will she listen to me? Still, maybe she'll see sense when you've tucked this one away safely in the jail. Have you got him on something this time? Tell me you've got him on something that'll put him away for a good long time.'

'Mum!' the wife shouted. 'For God's sake. Peacock's

only helping Duncan with his inquiries. Get back into the living room.'

The mother-in-law gave McFadgen a conspiratorial look and then started fighting her way past the dress and towards the door again.

'Lock him up and throw away the key,' she shouted as she departed. 'That's what I'd do with him. You're complicit in destroying my daughter's future if you don't, officer. Keep that in mind.'

Bev looked up towards the ceiling and shook her head, muttering something under her breath to try and keep a lid on it. 'She's a constant embarrassment,' she said. 'Sorry about that, Duncan. I'll go and keep an eye on her.'

But your man McFadgen had different ideas. 'Hang on a wee minute, Beverley,' he said. 'I'm thinking maybe you could help me with something yourself. Close the door there and tell me about your dinner at Rogano's with Peacock the other night. Is it worth the money there? I've been thinking of taking Liz for her birthday, but I'm swithering. How did you find it?'

He shot me a look, no doubt keen to see if I seemed nervous, knowing I was on to his game. But he'd already confirmed the whole thing with her the other day, and I knew he was on to plums if he was hoping to lead her into slipping up on times, or the sequence of events, or my presence in the restaurant for the duration. I shrugged back at him to let him know he was wasting his time, as well as everybody else's – but as it turned out, he got more than even he'd been bargaining for. You pretty much always do with the wife. Standard practice.

'Oh God, I didn't tell you what happened, did I?' she said. 'Will I tell him, Peacock? Have you already told him?'

'Go ahead, hen,' I said. 'Wire right in.'

'You got there about half past seven?' McFadgen said. 'Is that right?' But his line of questioning was entirely lost on the wife; she was off on her own track, and there was no stopping her.

'It was so embarrassing!' she said. 'Wasn't it, Peacock? It's hardly the sort of place we're used to anyway, Duncan. I was already feeling a bit self-conscious as it was. I didn't think I would be – I was looking forward to it for ages and I thought I'd really enjoy myself, but I could feel people in there looking at us right from the start. We were probably a bit overdressed – Peacock especially. I thought everybody in there would be done up, but everybody else looked quite boring really. Then I could tell that people thought we were probably talking too loud. I was just that excited, but I could feel myself getting a few looks. And the menu was a bit confusing. I kept making a fool of myself in front of the waitress, pronouncing things wrong.'

'You did fine, hen,' I told her. 'They're a bunch of stuck-up bastards in there, McFadgen. I'd give it a body swerve if I were you.'

'Don't listen to him, Duncan,' Bev said. 'Your wife'll

love it. And in the end they were lovely to us, absolutely lovely. I was just that embarrassed. Tell him what happened, Peacock.'

'You tell him, Bev,' I said. 'It's your story.'

'Oh God!' she said again, and her face flushed a colour close to that of the dress. 'We'd just finished our pudding, and I was absolutely stuffed, and we ordered some coffees and asked for the bill, and – I'll never forget it – I was just looking about in my bag for my lipstick when Peacock leant across the table towards me and whispered, "Have you got your purse in there, Bev?" "I thought this was your treat," I said, because that's what he'd told me. "This is my treat, Bev," he'd said. "Have whatever you like. Happy Anniversary." Now it turns out he's asking me if I've got my purse, and when I looked up at him I could tell he wasn't joking. "I've been dipped, Bev," he said. "My wallet's gone." Oh, *Duncan*! I could have ended myself. I really could. At first we thought he'd maybe just dropped his wallet, but he looked all over the restaurant and there was no sign of it. He'd paid for the drinks in the pub we went to before Rogano's, and that's the last place he'd had it. Somebody must have pinched it in there. And I didn't have my purse. I hadn't brought it with me. I thought I was going to boak my dinner back up right there and then, I really did.'

McFadgen's face was a picture. I gave him a wee wink, but he was far from amused. He looked as if somebody had just dunked his head in a bucket of cold water. Not too different from how the wife had looked in the very scene she was describing, in fact. That was McFadgen's wee porn-mag-receipt angle well and truly busted.

'You have to admit the staff could have been a lot worse about it, though, Peacock,' Bev said. 'I was sure they were going to think we were a couple of chancers, after the way we'd been sticking out like sore thumbs all night. I thought they'd imagine we'd pre-planned the whole thing. But when it came right down to it they were lovely. I'd had the idea that I could phone my pal Caroline to come round with her card and pay the bill for us. She just lives near by, on Ingram Street – you know the fancy flats up above the Italian Centre? I didn't even have a phone with me, but the waitress lent me hers and everything. I was nervous in case Caroline wouldn't be in, but she was, and she was there in a jiffy. Thank God. Oh, but what a night, Duncan. I was a nervous wreck by the end of it.'

You have to give it to McFadgen – defeated as he appeared to be, he was still doing his job all the way to the end.

'And what time was this, Beverley,' he said, 'when you finally got out of there?'

'It was nearly half nine,' the wife said, finishing him off completely. 'I felt bad about bringing Caroline out as late as that, but she was fine about it. And we went for a quick drink with her before we headed home, and she gave us some money for a taxi. We paid her back everything the next day, right enough.'

'Beverley!' the mother-in-law shouted from the living room then. 'Come and see this!'

The wife rolled her eyes and gathered up her skirts. 'You'd better excuse me,' she said. 'But take your wife there, Duncan. Really. She'll love it. Just remember to bring your wallet.'

She tugged at the door and set about bundling herself through it. 'Oh,' she said, 'and see if you can have a word with the fashion police about this dress, Duncan. See if they can't do anything about closing that wedding of Wilma's down. You press him on that, Peacock, do you hear me?'

And then she was gone.

'Are you wanting that beer now, Dunkie boy?' I said. 'I have to admit, you're fair looking as if you could use it.'

But he was already buttoning up his jacket, looking for the emergency exit.

'This is a stitch-up, Johnson,' he said. 'You know I know it's a stitch-up, and you know I know I'll get you in the end.'

I held the door open for him, and guided him out into the hall with a light hand on the elbow.

'It's certainly an *attempt* at a stitch-up,' I told him, 'but you're the one holding the needle, pal. You went through the records to find out that was my bank card without even bothering to notice I'd cancelled the thing on Thursday night, as soon as I realised it was gone. That smacks of a man trying to back up his prejudices at any cost if you ask me. Have another swatch at the data when you get back to the station. You'll see the cost of that transaction you're carrying the receipt for has been repaid into my account in full, reimbursed by the bank themselves.'

'Aye,' he muttered as a burst of madness came floating out of the living room, 'very convenient, Peacock. Very convenient indeed.'

It wasn't entirely clear what the wife and her mother were getting up to now. From the sounds of it, they were possibly chasing a bird that had flown in through an open window, hurling abuse at it, while it knocked down everything in its path. Either that, or the mother was trying to help Bev remove the bridesmaid's dress and it had all gone distinctly pear-shaped.

'You'll probably be doing me a favour, McFadgen – if you ever manage to put me in the jail,' I said. 'Listen to what I'm going back in amongst now. The peace and quiet of a prison cell might come as a welcome relief.'

'I'll be obliging you on that front soon enough,' he said. 'Watch and see if I don't. I'm on to you this time, Johnson – big time. And there's no way I'm letting go.'

He pulled the front door open and started clattering his way down through the close while I stood leaning over the banister, watching him go.

'McFadgen,' I shouted, when he reached the first-floor landing, and he stopped briefly and looked back up at me.

'Do yourself a favour, pal – lay off those Ian Rankin stories for a while. You're driving yourself daft, son. They're just books. Fairy tales for grown-ups. You'll end up giving yourself a cerebral haemorrhage.'

He shook his head and carried on his merry way, his big mad shoes echoing like gunshots in the close. Then he disappeared from view and I headed back inside at a leisurely pace, not in any desperate rush to find out what pandemonium awaited me.

3

I have to admit, this upcoming wedding is a godsend for me. I'm over the moon that it's happening, even if it does mean a fortnight of bedlam in the run-up to the wife's debut as a bridesmaid.

I mean, I'm hardly the biggest fan of weddings, and this one in particular falls some way short of being the match of the century. The bride, you've probably already gleaned, is a pal of the wife's – Wilma Caldwell. Wilma, in her turn, used to be married to an old pal of mine, Brian Caldwell, many moons ago now. There was some speculation regarding the paternity of their second wean, way back in the day, and that pretty much put the kibosh on love's young dream as far as Brian was concerned.

The groom, on the other hand, is something of an unknown quantity. Vince Cowie he's called. I've bumped into him here and there over the years; he's into a bit of this and a bit of that, much like myself. He's hardly a looker from what I remember, but he's a good fifteen years younger than Wilma, and that's probably enough to make up for his lack of conventional aesthetic appeal. Fair play to them both, that's my attitude to the union. There's been a wee bit of whispering here and there about the age gap but, like I say, I've got something of a vested interest in their getting together, so far be it from me to do anything other than wish them all the luck in the world.

You see, just about as soon as the ink dries on their marriage certificate, I'll be free and clear to roll out my latest money-making venture. I'll be fully at liberty to unleash my latest brainwave on the world. And is this *ever* a brainwave. Fuck me – it's an absolute belter. An absolute cert. And it's destined to have me up to my eyeballs in money by the end of the year.

I'll be rolling in the stuff.

So you'd better believe I'll be the first one with my glass in the air the minute the best man asks us to toast their coming together in holy matrimony.

Here's the fly in the ointment, though, the potential spanner in the works. It's fucking McFadgen, isn't it? I've got a fair bit of work to put in getting my venture ready to go between now and then, and it's proving somewhat difficult with the brave detective constantly at me, night and day.

My idea, you see, isn't strictly on the up and up. It falls somewhat squarely on the wrong side of the law. Which makes it fairly difficult to make any progress as long as McFadgen's two or three feet behind me for the best part of the day. He's starting to cramp my style a bit, if you get my meaning.

So I decided, the day after his delightful visit to the flat, that there was really only one thing for it. It was time to bite the bullet and pay a quick visit to John Jack, to see what nugget of information he could give me that might help my cause. John Jack's the de facto expert on the comings and goings of the shadier side of the city, and if he had a lead on somebody with more motive to have killed Dougie Dowds than me, I could hopefully send McFadgen off on that trail for the time being, and earn myself a bit of breathing space to attend to the matters currently closest to my heart.

I got the feeling, the minute I stepped into John Jack's office, that he wasn't all that pleased to see me.

It was just minor things, subtle hints I picked up – the way his eyes narrowed as he turned towards the door when I came in, the lack of a welcoming smile, the manner in which he dropped his pen down on his desk and said, 'Aww for fuck's sake, Peacock. Not you. Not today. I'm not in the mood.'

Like I say – subtle hints. I'm a sensitive man, and I pick up on these social cues.

Still, I persevered.

John Jack's office is upstairs from the casino he owns, and now and again the odds turn against him down there. He's also a big fan of the snooker and the darts, and things going in the opposite direction from the one he wants them to go in a match can have a profound effect on his mood. I saw his telly was showing a darts match right at the minute, with the sound turned down, so I decided not to take his deficiencies as a host personally. It was likely I'd just walked in at a bad time, and I was bearing the brunt of his frustration.

'What's the problem, John?' I said as I plonked myself down on the leather sofa at the back wall. 'What's getting in about you this morning?'

He took a long deep breath, and then looked me squarely in the eye.

'You are,' he said. 'I was feeling tip top for once. Frankie's up in the darts. Everything's quiet downstairs. Even my ulcer's taken a break and eased off on the gyp it's been giving me. Then I hear a knock on my door. "Who's this?" I say to myself. "My daughter bringing me an early lunch? Rab Campbell turning up with some insider knowledge he's gleaned from the stables about the two-thirty at Haymarket?" Is it hell as like. In you wander, and down come my modest hopes. Are you bringing me an early lunch? Are you offering me a dead cert in the two-thirty? Are you buggery. You're after something for yourself. Investment in another one of your demented ideas, more likely than not. I'm not interested, Peacock. Whatever it is, I'm not interested. I've lost more money on your idiotic nonsense than I've lost on all my other gambling put together. So you can take it elsewhere. Take it to some other mug. And close the door on your way out.'

I held my tongue. It seemed I'd been slightly off in my earlier assessment of what had been eating him. Misread the situation somewhat. So I let his blood pressure settle, and then I straightened myself up on the couch.

'Are you finished?' I asked him, and his eyes widened.

'Am I *what*?'

'Finished,' I said. 'Ranting. Are you feeling better, now you've said your piece? You're a hell of a host, John. Oh, and by the way, you're way off. I'm not here looking for investment. If you remember right, you already turned down my latest stormer. And it's coming along fine without your meddling in it. More than fine. This is the jackpot, John. This is the big time. And you've dealt your future net worth a severe blow by passing on it. Fair enough. Your choice. But I'm not here looking for funding. This beauty'll keep me occupied for the foreseeable. Fully occupied.'

He looked as if somebody was holding a bit of paper smeared with dog shit under his nose, and stared at me through that expression for a good ten seconds.

'That *fingerprint* mince?' he said. 'Is that what we're talking about here? You're still hellbent on that? Are you *serious*?'

'Serious as a heart attack, John,' I said. 'We're up and running. Just waiting on the get go.'

'Brian Caldwell went for that?' he said. 'Honestly? Christ Almighty, I sent you to him as a *joke*, Peacock. It's one of the shittiest ideas I've heard in my puff. And I've heard my fair share of howlers, mainly from you. You're absolutely serious? Caldwell went for that?'

'He's a man of vision,' I said. 'Unlike yourself. I mean, fair play, you've had your moments in the past. You've seen the potential in my genius here and there. But you sorely misjudged this one. This is my ticket, John. And Brian could see it's his ticket as well. Short-sightedness, that's your problem, John. You're all about the big return, in double quick time. And I admit I've fallen victim to that way of thinking myself in the past. The boom and the bust. But what I'm setting up here is a long-term income stream. That's the future, John – constant payments over the long term. That's what you've missed out on with this one. Still, let bygones be bygones. You've fucked up and you've moved on. Let's leave it at that. Suffice to say, I'm not here looking for investment. You can take the strain off that ulcer for the time being, in case it perforates.'

After that, I gave myself peace for a wee while. I'd just remembered that John Jack was essentially right in his assumptions, that I *had* come there to ask him for something, even if it wasn't money. So I let my thinking apparatus tick over, and looked for a method to make it seem otherwise.

'Right,' he said, giving the darts a quick glance and rubbing the back of his neck. 'I'm a busy man, Peacock. That's enough shite for one day. Let's just hear what you're wanting, and then I can get you out of here.'

I acted a bit offended at the suggestion that I was wanting something, just to buy a tad more thinking time, then I was on it – the inspiration I'd been looking for appeared, and I got down to business.

'I'm tempted to just fuck off and leave you to it, John,' I said. 'Here I am, come to do you a good turn, and all I get is snash. Aspersions cast on my good name.' I stood up, and made out I was getting ready to leave. He seemed pretty nonplussed. 'I was just bringing you a bit of information, a hot bit of gossip from the underworld, but if you're not interested, if you'd rather be watching the darts . . .'

I'll tell you what, I didn't have to carry on with my charade of heading for the door after that – he was a changed man suddenly, all ears. That's just how it is with John Jack. It's a bit like putting a tumbler of whisky in front of a thirsty alcoholic – all decorum goes out the window.

'What have you got?' he asked me, practically slevering. The eyes were pleading, the fists bunched up. It was hard not to be touched by the man's childlike excitement.

'Have you heard about the thing Jinky's putting together?' I asked him, and he shook his head at speed, hardly able to contain himself.

'Naw,' he said. 'What?'

So I told him about a job my pal Jinky had been banging on about in the Horseshoe Bar a couple of nights previously. It was nothing much, a minor smash and grab he was looking to recruit a couple of bodies for – but that's the beauty of John Jack's obsession. He doesn't discriminate. Whether it's a trifling disagreement between a couple of folk he knows, or a major plot to bring the government to its knees, he values it all exactly the same. It all contributes to him keeping tabs on the city as a whole – it's all a part of the big picture. And having the biggest, most accurate picture he can possibly have is his number one priority.

He grabbed his notebook out of a desk drawer and asked me a few probing questions as he scribbled at a rate of knots. From where I was sitting, the paper looked like it was in severe danger of bursting into flames, but eventually he appeared to be satisfied that he'd everything committed to record, and while he was reading it back over I decided it was time to make my play.

'Those notebooks of yours must be able to answer some amount of questions,' I said. 'Is there anything you don't know about what's going on in Glasgow, John?'

'Very little,' he said.

'You should apply to go on *Mastermind*. Specialist subject: The Ins and Outs of the Glasgow Underworld. Incorporating various surrounding areas. Nineteen ninety-six until the present moment.'

'Very funny,' he said, without laughing, and he tucked his notebook back in the drawer, looking like a junkie who's just had his fix.

'I'd better hit the trail,' I said. 'Meeting the wife for lunch near her work.'

I eased myself up off the couch and then acted as if I'd just been struck by an afterthought. 'Oh, by the way, what have you heard about this Dougie Dowds business? That was a hell of a thing. Any word on who was responsible for that?'

'Eh?' he said. His face had changed. Startled, I suppose, you'd call the look on it.

'Dougie Dowds,' I repeated. 'I'm just asking if you know who whacked the poor wee bastard. Any news?'

He added a deep frown to the startled expression. It was a hell of a combination. His face hardly knew if it was coming or going. And then he said, '*You* did. It was you that did that. Obviously.'

A flush of embarrassment found its place on the highly crowded landscape of the big man's face.

I sat back down on the couch and stared at him. 'How come? Where are you getting that from?'

'McFadgen,' he said. 'Adam Stevenson says McFadgen gave him a right good grilling about you. Same thing with Bert Hamilton. Willy Sooter says McFadgen's ruled out the possibility of it being anybody else but you – he's done considering any other options. McFadgen's rarely wrong, Peacock. In my experience.'

'McFadgen's a chump,' I said.

Things didn't look good. The hope that J.J. would at least have heard whisperings of another tumshie I could send McFadgen off to take a look at had hit a brick wall. But my synapses were in fine form, and an alternative approach suddenly struck me.

'Tell me this, John,' I said. 'Who swiped thon painting from Pollok House last month? The Spanish thing. Any word on that?'

The complicated weather had cleared on the Jackster's map, and he just studied me with a look of certainty now.

'That was you as well,' he said. 'Had to be. I don't think anybody's in any doubt about that.'

'How?'

'Well, for one thing, who else but you could have got in there and back out with the thing? It's got you written all over it. You're a total prick in the main, but credit where it's due – I doubt there's anybody else in the city could have pulled that one off.'

I leant forward and rubbed my forehead. I appreciated the compliment, but it was hardly getting me any closer to my goal.

'Scratch that thing I said earlier about *Mastermind*, John,' I told him. 'On second thoughts it would be a hell of an episode. "Who did this?" "Peacock Johnson." "Who did that?" "Peacock Johnson." "Who . . . I've started so I'll finish." "Peacock Johnson." You're a bit of a stuck record at the minute, John. Have you been reading Ian Rankin recently, by any chance?'

'Who?'

'Forget it. Just a hunch. How about I hit you with another wee nugget of information? Are you up for that? Two for the price of one.'

The slevering started again, the wide eyes. He almost went so far as to stand up.

'Prepare yourself,' I said. 'Ready? Here's the lowdown, John . . . as much as I enjoyed you bumming up my breaking-and-entering skills, and as much as I appreciate the compliment, I never actually took that painting. I'd nothing to do with it.'

The notebook was back out on the desk again. He'd started flicking through the pages and uncapping his pen.

'Who was it?' he said, almost in a whisper.

I shrugged my shoulders. 'Haven't a Scooby. But according to McFadgen, Dougie Dowds was on his way to fill McFadgen in on the identity of the perpetrator when he got whacked. And I need McFadgen off my back, so's I can get on with putting this fingerprint operation into action. If I can put him on the trail of whoever took that painting, it should give me plenty of breathing space while he goes after whoever pinched the picture.'

I looked at the familiar hunger consuming the Jackster, his overwhelming need to *know*. A wee rip had just appeared in the fabric of his universe. He'd thought he had everything all ordered and in place – the Pollok House theft probably the furthest thing from his mind, because he had it all shipshape and accounted for. Now he needed resolution all over again – closure on the gap that had just opened up in his knowledge.

Either that, or he'd eaten a decidedly dodgy oyster for breakfast, and was in urgent need of getting to a toilet. The boy was in a severe state of agitation.

'You think you can find out who swiped that picture?' I asked him, while he flicked through his phone book in something of a panic.

That was when I realised I'd overplayed my hand, or at least got a bit premature with myself. He stopped flicking, and looked up at me without bothering to raise his head.

'Wait a minute,' he said. 'Is that what all of this has been about? All along? Is this what you came here for in the first place? To find out if I knew who swiped that painting?'

I got up and walked across the room towards his desk, busted. 'I actually came to see what the line-up looked liked in terms of who whacked Dougie Dowds. I gave you more credit for being up to speed on that than you actually deserved. You're slipping, John, as far as I can see. The painting angle's a fallback – a quick improvisation. Besides, you owe me it – for the Jinky data. And for setting you right regarding your misapprehensions about who stole the picture in the first place.'

He grunted. A dismissive grunt. He opened his contacts book again and went back to fucking about in there, at high speed.

'To answer your original question,' he said, 'aye, I'll be able to find out who took the painting. As far as me putting any of the information your way goes – you can whistle for it. I don't like being taken for a mug. Close the door on your way out.'

I stayed exactly where I was, leaning on his desk, staring out the window behind him.

'Look at it this way, John,' I said, 'as long as I've got McFadgen constantly breathing down my neck, the fingerprint idea's up the spout. And the longer that's on hold, the more likely I am to come up with another idea – and you know what happens whenever I come up with an idea. I come to you looking for money to float it. And nine times out of ten, the idea's a peach and you go for it. And nine times out of ten something happens to make the idea fall flat on its arse, taking your investment with it. You see what I'm saying? That's the type of scenario you're leaving yourself open to if you keep the information to yourself. You'll be hurting yourself.'

He deigned to employ the grunt again. 'Not if McFadgen does his job properly. If he locks you up I'll be shot of you for good. You *and* your ideas.'

You have to hand it to the Jackster sometimes – he's a hard nut to crack. Sometimes you have to drill right down into the nitty gritty, take it all the way. So that's exactly what I did. The man hadn't left me any other option.

'Here's the thing, though, John,' I said, and I rapped my knuckles on his desk. 'McFadgen's got a daft idea in his head, and it's this: he's convinced himself that the reason I knew Dougie Dowds was on his way to tell him who stole the painting is because *you* told me that was the case. He's well aware of your reputation for knowing everything. Now, the way I see it, he's overlooking something, in his zeal to see me behind bars. His unhealthy obsession's blinded him to an obvious conclusion he *could* have drawn from his flawed thesis – namely, that if you knew what Dougie Dowds was just about to do, it might well have been *you* that had a vested interest in making sure the information didn't reach McFadgen. And it might well have been *you* that took steps to prevent that happening.'

'Pish,' he said. 'Utter pish. I don't know *who* took the painting. We've established that.'

'*We've* established that,' I said. 'But if I pointed out to McFadgen that he might be overlooking the obvious, he'd start snooping around you for a while to explore the possibility. He'd be paying you a visit or two, asking you some awkward questions. Mind you, maybe you're as clean as a whistle, business-wise. Maybe I'm barking up the wrong tree. Maybe you'd be quite happy to entertain him round here of an afternoon. Is that the case?'

Was it hell as like.

'You're a slimy bastard, Peacock,' he said, but I refused to let it get to me.

'How long do you think it'll take you to have a few names regarding the painting?' I asked him. 'If I drop in about two bells tomorrow afternoon, how does that sound?'

He never answered, but I knew his desire to know the names himself would have uncovered enough for me to be getting on with well before that.

'I'll see you about two, John,' I said, and then I headed for the door. He called me something under his breath as I drew the thing shut behind me, but I'll spare you the finer details of his habitual tendency to abuse the vernacular.

4

Once upon a time, probably five or six years past, I'd a pal by the name of Tam Bailey. Well, I say a pal – I suppose our relationship was really more of an enforced acquaintance. This was back when John Jack was big on putting teams together, and Tam happened to be part of one of those teams.

Anyway, that's as may be, here's the point: I gradually started to notice, during the five or six weeks I spent in Tam's company, that whenever I'd been wearing a particularly eye-catching pair of shoes for a couple of days, or a sharp new shirt, Tam would pay me a compliment on the item in question and ask me where I'd got it. Then, lo and behold, he'd turn up one morning wearing the same thing himself.

I mean, what do you say to somebody in a situation like that? You've probably already gathered I take a particular pride in my appearance. I like to stand out from the crowd. But when the crowd starts copying your every move, it makes it harder and harder to achieve that objective. At the same time, you're likely to come across as a bit of a bawbag if, when someone comes up to you and says, 'What do you think of the shoes, Peacock?' you reply to the effect that you – and only you – are entitled to be sporting that particular style of moccasin.

You see my dilemma?

It became a right puzzler for me. And it got thoroughly in about me until it reached the point where it was keeping me awake at night – tormented. I felt as if I was losing my individual identity. I felt as if I was fading away. Every time I found myself standing beside this clown, wearing the same kit I was wearing, I felt like I only half existed.

As an initial stopgap, I stepped up my rate of consumption – trying to keep ahead of the boy by acquiring a new outfit every few days. But he was totally up for that. It only worked momentarily, and then he changed his speed to match mine and I was back to square one again.

Part of the problem, if I'm being perfectly honest, was that Tam was hardly the shapeliest of fellows. He was more or less built like a brick shithouse and, in my own humble opinion, there were very few outfits he could actually carry off. And it started to affect my confidence, on top of everything else, wondering if that might be how *I* actually looked. Wondering if that might be how the gear actually looked on me.

But like I say, I'm an ideas man. If I let the back bit of my brain chew on a problem for long enough, it's guaranteed to throw up a solution sooner or later. And in this particular instance I came up with a blinder, a real screamer. And it hit me just as I was waking up one morning, just at the very instant I was starting to get down about the prospect of tooling about the city with my doppelgänger in tow again, with every third passer-by doing a double take, wondering what the hell we were playing at.

'Move it up a stage.' That's what the voice told me. 'Take it to the next level, Peacock.'

And I knew instantly that it would work. I sprang out of bed like a new man, skipped breakfast, and made straight for Buchanan Street.

Designer labels, that was the answer – threads so outrageously expensive that Tam couldn't afford to follow me. Six hundred quid shoes, shirts that cost the same as a week in Spain, a leather jacket worth as much as a secondhand car.

And it worked.

'I like the jeans,' Tam said that afternoon. 'Where did you dig them up?'

And I told him. No problem. But the next morning he came in kind of ashen-faced, wearing the same pair of cords he'd had on the day before, and he asked about my tanktop instead.

I was bulletproof. Back to my old self. A one-off on the city streets.

Granted, I just about bankrupted myself. I had to take a chunk of equity out the flat to meet the next few months' expenses. But Tam was back where he belonged, consigned to the grey masses, dicking about with the pigeons in his jeans and his sweatshirts.

But here's the long-term damage that's resulted: once you've tasted that stuff, you can never go back. Once you've strutted about in Versace and Armani and Dolce & Gabbana, you're hardly going to go back to the high street. It's like moving on to heroin – a few aspirins in a can of Coke can no longer do the job.

So to cut a long story short, I'm now a junkie for the designer rags. On occasion, some vintage item'll still more or less do it for me, but barring that I'm a slave to the names. Which has taken me to the edge of financial ruin on more than a few occasions. It's an expensive habit, no doubt about that.

And directly after leaving John Jack's office, as I made my way through the town to my lunch date with the wife I fell prey to temptation yet again. I was making good time, all set to reach the point of rendezvous before Bev was likely to arrive, when I saw a cracking-looking suit in a window on Buchanan Street – the very thing that would be ideal for this upcoming wedding. Olive green, with pink cuffs and a pink collar, patterned with dark green and red swirls – the whole shebang courtesy of Prada.

I'll tell you, I was like a moth drawn towards a light bulb.

I clocked it from fifty yards away, and it pulled me across the cobbles at high speed, careering into passers-by without even noticing they were there. And I stood with my nose pressed against the glass, bewitched – practically salivating.

'Treat yourself,' a wee voice in my bonce whispered. 'This wedding's a big celebration for you. The start of a new life. Go for it, pal.'

So I nipped inside and had a look at the price tag. Fucking astro*nomical*. Cata*strophically* expensive.

Still, I couldn't see any harm in at least trying it on. And I did. And it looked good. I was just experiencing the familiar sweats, struggling against the impulse to bankrupt us again, and wondering how I would explain it to the wife, when I suddenly remembered I was meant to be with the wife that very minute. I consulted the watch and realised I was on course to be a good ten minutes late now, if I didn't make a sprint for it, and that was enough to get me to ditch the shopping spree for the time being.

'You can come and try it on again when Bev's back at her work,' I told myself as I returned it sadly to the racks. Then I belted up Sauchiehall Street and found her sitting in the designated eatery with a face like fizz.

'You're fifteen minutes late,' she shouted, before I'd even reached the table. Conversations came to a halt all over the restaurant; folk swivelled in their chairs to get a right good look at me. 'What are you playing at?' Bev carried on.

'I've only got forty-five minutes left, Peacock. I told you not to be late. Where the hell have you been?'

I nodded and pulled up a chair. 'I'm sorry, hen,' I said. 'I got held up looking at a . . .'

But that was as far as I got. Apparently it was a rhetorical question, and she fired a menu across the table at me, disrupting the arrangement of napkins and cutlery that had been laid out at my place.

'Just pick something quickly,' she said. 'The first thing you see. No way am I missing out on the breadsticks and chocolate dip for dessert, Peacock. I told you that's how I wanted to come here. Now I'm going to have to bolt my main course just to have any chance of getting them in time. Have you found something? I'm having the linguine with the mushroom sauce. What are you getting?'

I'd barely had a chance to open the menu, never mind peruse the options. And I'll be honest with you, the couple of things I'd managed to take a swatch at hardly filled me with much enthusiasm.

'Is there a roll and fried egg on here,' I said, but she was looking past me, signalling to a waitress to come and serve us. 'I could murder a roll and fried egg, Bev.'

'I could murder you,' she said. 'Don't you dare embarrass me in front of this lassie. This is a classy place, Peacock. Get the fusilli. I had that when I came with Janice. Tomato and garlic sauce. It's gorgeous.'

The menu was starting to blur.

'Hi,' the wife said, all sweetness and light now. The waitress had appeared, and she started running through her spiel about specials and dishes of the day, but the wife cut her short.

'We're in a bit of a hurry, unfortunately,' she said. 'Owing to this one turning up half an hour late. But I really want to make it to the breadsticks and chocolate dip for dessert. Have you got the breadsticks today?'

The waitress was a tad rattled at being interrupted mid-flow, but she put a brave face on it and assured the wife they had breadsticks and chocolate aplenty.

'Brilliant,' the wife said. 'Just bring me the linguine then, honey. No starters. Will it come quite quickly? I've only really got about forty minutes till I need to be back at work. I shouldn't really even be eating the breadsticks. I'm supposed to be on a diet – amn't I, Peacock? I'm a bridesmaid at my pal's wedding in a couple of weeks, and I was trying to lose weight for the occasion. Then I got a sneak preview of the dress I'm supposed to be wearing. Holy moly. What's it like, Peacock? I'll be a right state no matter how much weight I lose. So the diet's immaterial – I'm going for the breadsticks. How long does the linguine normally take to come, sweetheart?'

The poor wee lassie hardly knew if she was coming or going. 'Eh . . . just about ten minutes, I think,' she said. 'You should make it in time for the breadsticks. I'll tell them to be as quick as they can.'

The wife was satisfied, and the waitress turned her attentions to me. I was still doing battle with the menu, getting nowhere.

'What about yourself, sir?' the lassie said. 'Are you ready to order?'

'Of course he's ready,' Bev chipped in. 'What are you having, Peacock? The fusilli?'

'What about a wee roll and fried egg?' I asked the waitress. 'Could you stretch to that? With a dod of brown sauce on the side?'

'Eh . . .' she said.

'God almighty!' the wife said. 'Of course they haven't got a roll and fried egg, Peacock. I swear to God, I can't take him anywhere, hen. I'm really sorry. You're embarrassing the life out of me here, Peacock.'

'We've got a pizza with a fried egg on it,' the waitress said. 'I could get you that.'

'A pizza?'

'Aye, with a fried egg on it.'

'That's sounds manky,' I said.

'It does not!' the wife said. 'You're an ignoramus, Peacock Johnson. Bring him that, darling. That sounds lovely.'

She handed her menu to the waitress, and the waitress looked at me questioningly – almost pleadingly.

'Fair enough,' I said, just to put the poor soul out of her misery. 'Bring me that. Whatever. And a wee beer. Have you got beer?'

She nodded, and made a break for it, no doubt deeply relieved to have escaped the madness that is the Johnson experience.

'How come we never just met up in the Pancake Place, Bev?' I said. 'I could have got a roll and fried egg in there, no problem. That would have done me nicely.'

'Are you serious?'

'Aye, how?'

'Because, Peacock, the Pancake Place closed. Five years ago.'

'How come? That was a great place. What did it close for?'

She took a deep breath. 'I think I've got a bit more to worry about right at this minute than why the Pancake Place closed down, Peacock. Don't you?'

'Like what?'

'The *wedding*,' she said. 'That *dress*. Have you even been listening to me? I swear to God it's like talking to the wall sometimes. What did you *think* I was talking about?'

My immediate impulse was to say, 'When?' I could have sworn for the life of me that all we'd been talking about was my fried egg roll, but I let it go. I knew from past experience the 'When?' would lead me nowhere, so I just told her to carry on.

'I was telling Claire about it in work this morning,' she said. 'She thought I was winding her up till I showed her the picture on my phone. She says . . . You know Claire, don't you?'

'The one that lost her rabbit?'

'That was Wendy. Claire's the one with the stepson. You met her at Liam Grant's barbecue. She'd a blue jumpsuit on.'

'Aww.'

'Or maybe that was another time. Never mind. I'm sure you've met her somewhere. She's got a stepson. Alfie. Or maybe he's called Craig. I think it's Craig. He's seven or eight. I've been talking to her about this dress all morning. I think it's on the verge of giving me a nervous breakdown, Peacock, I really do. Claire says . . . Oh, wait till you hear what happened to her. You're not going to believe this. It's really awful.'

And off she went into a story about this Claire body, which as far as I could ascertain involved a golf course, a coupon off the internet for a cheap night in a hotel in Dunfermline, and a welly boot. How it all slotted together I couldn't even begin to tell you. I think I slipped in and out of consciousness at least twice, and I got caught up in trying to remember if I'd *ever* been to a barbecue, with anybody, when I should probably have been giving my full attention to how the hotel coupon and the welly boot had come to be in the same story.

If, in fact, they *were* part of the same story.

To tell the truth, I was starting to feel as if I was on the verge of a nervous breakdown myself as the thing progressed. There even seemed to be a meerkat involved at one point, but I'm perfectly willing to believe that was an image I retrieved from a dream as I slipped in and out of my coma.

'Is that not terrible?' Bev said in the end. 'Can you believe that? How can that even happen to a person? I didn't know what to tell her. What would you have told her to do?'

Thankfully, the waitress reappeared at this point, heavily weighed down by our respective orders. She plonked the pasta in front of Bev, and Bev started cooing indulgently.

'Oh my!' she said. 'Look at that, Peacock. Does that not look gorgeous? Thanks very much, honey. Oh, that looks amazing.'

It was more than I could say for mine. To me, mine just looked like a waste of a good fried egg. Not to mention downright weird. It was definitely a pizza, no doubt about that – but the fried egg was just sitting there bang smack on top of it. Right in the middle of the thing.

'Parmesan?' the waitress said to the wife, and the wife nodded big style. She was obliged to nod owing to the fact that her mouth was already stuffed full with the linguine, and the waitress started shaving cheese into the bowl with the wife still grabbing mouthfuls of the stuff round about her.

'For you, sir?' the waitress said, but I gave it a by. I'd a notion that cheese scraped onto the fried egg would only add to the chaos.

'Can I get anything else for either of you?' the waitress asked, and Bev chewed furiously.

'Just line up those breadsticks ready,' she said. 'We'll be

finished in a jiffy. This pasta is absolutely delicious. I'll be making short work of this.'

'I've already got the breadsticks laid out in the kitchen,' the waitress said. 'Enjoy your meals.'

And then she sauntered off, leaving us to it.

As manky as the pizza looked, I couldn't help but feel I owed it a debt of gratitude. Its arrival had managed to move the story about Dunfermline, and the request for my response to it, right off the agenda. And as I poked at the egg yolk with my knife, to test how hard it was, I decided to kickstart the next segment of the conversation myself, in case we inadvertently drifted back to Claire and her internet coupon again.

'How come you don't just tell her?' I said.

'Who? Tell who what? What the hell are you on about, Peacock?'

'Wilma,' I said. 'The bride. How come you don't just tell her?'

'Tell her what?'

'That you don't like the dress. Just tell her you don't want to wear it. What's the problem, Bev?'

'Oh for God's sake,' she said. 'Grow up, Peacock. Are you mental? A couple of weeks ago I told her I wasn't too sure about the font she'd used on the invitations. She burst into tears and it took me an hour and a half to get her out the bathroom. Then when I asked her who recommended the caterer she's using – quite innocently, mind you – she accused me of trying to sabotage her big day, out of jealousy. Can you imagine her reaction if I tried to criticise her choice of bridesmaids' dresses? She'd probably hurl herself off the Kingston Bridge. Or hurl me off it. Her sanity's hanging by a delicate thread, Peacock.'

She looked at her watch. 'Get a move on with that pizza. The clock's ticking here. I'm nearly finished mine and you're hardly even started. Come on, chop chop. Your late arrival better not hamper my appointment with those breadsticks, I'm telling you. What kept you anyway? You promised me you wouldn't be late.'

'I lost track of the time,' I told her. 'I was looking at a suit for the wedding. I think I need your help there, Bev. It's way out of the price range, but I'm finding it hard to . . .'

Her phone buzzed.

'Oh God,' she said. 'I'll bet that's a text from my boss. See if he needs me back early . . .'

She picked up her bag and started fishing about in it till she located her specs, then she squinted at the screen of the phone through them, still shovelling the pasta in as she read.

'It's a Prada suit, hen,' I said. 'It costs a bomb, but I'm sorely tempted. It's giving me the sweats. I think I might need you to go in there and . . .'

She held up her hand. 'It's the bride-to-be,' she said. 'Talk of the Devil. I'd better answer this, Peacock. She's got herself in a right flap. Get to work on that pizza, I'll just be a minute.'

The wee thumb of fury went into action as she held the phone up in front of her with one hand and forked away at the pasta with the other.

The waitress drifted by and asked if everything was all right and could she get us anything else.

The wife told her she was fine. I waited till she was fully engrossed in her typing again, and then whispered to the lassie to bring us a wee basket of bread, if it wasn't too much trouble. By the time Bev finally laid her phone back down on the table, I'd the fried egg between two suitable slices and I was starting to feel a bit more human again. It was a tad lacking without any brown sauce, but the yolk was soft enough to keep the whole thing from being prohibitively dry.

The wife didn't even clock it. She was so wrapped up in whatever had been going down between herself and Wilma that the whole enterprise went blissfully undetected.

She chewed quietly on the remainder of her linguine, staring off into space with a slight frown on her face, still wearing the reading glasses – her eyes comically magnified by the lenses.

'About this suit, Bev,' I said after a while. 'I was thinking you could maybe come and take a look at it. After work or something.'

'Eh . . .' she said. 'Oh . . .' She peeled the specs off and shoved them in her bag. 'Wilma says she's got the jitters. She says she's having second thoughts.'

'About the dresses?'

'The what?'

'The dresses. She's having second thoughts about the dresses?'

'What dresses?'

'*Your* dresses.'

'My . . .? Oh. No. About the whole thing. About the wedding. She wants me to go round there after work to help her work out what to do. She says she's got the jitters. She's freaking out about the commitment.'

The fried egg suddenly didn't taste quite as magnificent as it had a minute before. In fact, it had more or less turned to ashes on my tongue, as I've heard them say. A far from pleasant experience.

I shoved the rest of it in and just swallowed it whole. 'She's pulling out?' I said. 'For real?'

'She seems to be thinking about it,' the wife said. 'She sounds in a right mess.'

'What did you tell her?' I asked. 'Did you tell her it's just normal? Last-minute doubts. It's pretty normal, eh?'

'I told her not to do anything hasty. I told her we'd have a right good talk about it tonight. When I'm finished work.'

This was big – I had to admit that. In fact, it was a full-on nuclear disaster. If Wilma went through with her mad plan and cancelled the wedding, I'd be fucked. My entire livelihood relied on this wedding going ahead. No two ways about it.

'Oh, look at your *plate*,' Bev said then. 'Peacock, you've still hardly started.' She reached across the table and tore a chunk out of my pizza, and stuck it on her own plate.

'What's keeping you?' she said. 'Come on, hurry up!'

'I think I've lost my appetite,' I said, and she wolfed down the bit of pizza she'd pinched. Then she looked about the place for the waitress and waved her over.

'Can you just bring me my breadsticks while he's still eating?' she said. 'He's driving me daft. I'll never make it back to work in time if I don't get started on them now.'

'Not a problem,' the waitress said. 'Did you enjoy the linguine? Was it okay for you?'

'It was divine,' the wife said. 'Absolutely delicious.'

The waitress picked up Bev's plate and her cutlery. 'I'll be right back,' she said, and she was as good as her word. In two shakes there was a mug full of sugar-coated breadsticks sitting in front of the wife, and a big dish of dipping chocolate, and she was looking like a wean on Christmas morning.

'Oh my God!' she said. 'Look at this, Peacock. Look at it. Can you believe it? Here, have one. You can go back to your pizza in a minute. Try one of these first. Just try it.'

She held one of the sticks out to me, and I took it just to get peace.

'Dip it in the chocolate,' she said. 'Come on. I had these that time I was here with Janice. Last month. Oh, you're going to love these, Peacock. Here.'

She held the dish of chocolate out to me and waved it about.

'Maybe in a minute, Bev,' I said. 'I told you, I'm struggling a bit at the minute. I've lost my appetite.'

'How?'

'The news about Wilma, thinking of cancelling the wedding. It's shaken me up.'

'Aww, you're an old romantic, Peacock. I knew it. I'm always saying that, amn't I? You try and cover it up, but I can see it. That's what I'm always telling Mum. If only she could see you now. Wee Peacock. Off his dinner. It'll be fine. Don't worry about it. I'll talk to Wilma tonight and everything'll be fine. Now . . .'

She gave up on wiggling the dipping chocolate beneath my nose and plonked it back down on the table. Then she carefully selected a breadstick from the mug, swithering between two of the longest ones for a bit. And when she was happy, she dipped the tip of her selection into the chocolate sauce, fired the thing into her mouth, and closed her eyes.

'Ohhh . . .' she shouted, 'Oh God! That is *heaven*.'

She stuck the remaining half into the chocolate and downed that, then she picked up another stick and went through the whole routine again.

'Here,' she said, picking up the chocolate dish for a second time. 'I'm not taking no for an answer again, Peacock. Get that in the chocolate and try it. It's out of this world.'

We'd a wee audience observing us by this point, so I whacked the breadstick into the sauce just to calm her down, and she stared at me searchingly as I took a bite of the thing.

'Well?' she said. 'Impressed?'

I have to admit, it was pretty special. 'Aye,' I said, 'not bad at all, hen. Very nice.'

She dealt herself another one. Same rigmarole. The closed eyes, the inappropriate moaning, the muttered praise. But then, before it was quite time to re-dip the second half, her eyes flew open and suddenly she was staring at me with a big grin.

'Chocolate inspiration,' she said. 'It's struck me. I've just had a brilliant idea.'

I perked up. I assumed it must be regarding the wedding – a way to get the bride back on the straight and narrow. I fired the second half of my own stick into the chocolate sauce, full of new hope, and got wired into it.

'What have you got, Bev?' I asked her. 'You're looking suitably mischievous, hen. What are we talking about here? What are you onto?'

'Listen to this,' she said, 'it's perfect. I'm off the hook. All I have to do is encourage Wilma's reservations – you know, back her up a bit, fill her in on a few examples of the misery you've caused me over the years, basically paint her a grim picture of marriage in general, and that hideous meringue of a dress and me'll be history. Exes. I told you these breadsticks had something special in them, didn't I?'

She held a new one up to the light as if she was trying to work out where the magic came from, and I felt like the ground had opened up beneath me.

'Don't do that, Bev!' I said. 'That's a rotten idea. It's brutal.'

She laughed a devilish laugh. 'I'm only joking,' she said. 'Well, half joking. It's just the chocolate talking. Probably. We'll see. See how things stand when I come back down to earth again. You have to admit, though, it's a pretty good opportunity.'

'Fair enough,' I said. 'But think of the groom. He's besotted, Bev. This would destroy him.'

'I thought you said you hardly knew him.'

'I don't. But Jinky knows him. That's what Jinky was saying. This relationship's saved his life, Bev. From what I hear.'

'From Jinky?'

'Aye, from Jinky. Listen, Bev, I'll think of a way to get you out of having to wear that dress. I'm an ideas man. It's what I do. I'll come up with a blinder, I promise. Just try and make sure you talk Wilma down off the ledge tonight, eh? For the groom's sake? Come on, Bev – have a heart.'

She looked at me suspiciously. 'What's going on here, Peacock? What are you up to? Have you got something going on with this wedding?'

'Like what?'

'Hmmm . . .' she said. 'You're up to something. I'd put a bet on it.'

'You're havering,' I said.

She looked at her watch and jumped. 'Oh, God. Right, I'd better get going.'

She threw her phone into her bag and crammed one last breadstick into her mouth, then she stood up. 'You'll have to pay. Have you got your wallet this time?'

I checked to make sure and gave her the nod, and she leant in towards me and kissed flakes of breadstick all over my cheek.

'You'll have to get your own dinner tonight,' she said. 'I'll be at Wilma's.'

'Just make sure you give her the right advice,' I said.

'I'll see,' she said. 'I'll have to wait till I come down off this chocolate cloud to find out what I'm really thinking.'

'I'm serious, Bev,' I said, but she was already gone, legging it towards the door.

'You be sure and leave that girl a proper tip,' she shouted before she left.

'Did you enjoy the breadsticks?' the waitress shouted after her.

'Out of this world, darling,' the wife shouted back. 'Totally orgasmic.'

And then she disappeared out onto the street, leaving a good whack of our fellow diners staring after her as she went.

She's some boy, the wife.

I was in a bit of a state after she left, I'm not going to sit here and lie to you. The thought that she might nudge Wilma towards calling off the wedding got right in about me. I tried to tell myself it was far from likely, but the worst of it was, I wouldn't really have put it past her. Not really.

I was just about a nervous wreck by the time the waitress appeared, asking if she could get me anything else.

'Aww, aye . . . naw . . .' I said. 'Just the bill, hen. Just bring me the bill.'

'Absolutely,' she said, and she started clearing stuff away.

'Come to think of it,' I said, 'could you put that pizza in a box for me? I'll take it away and heat it up for my tea.'

'Not a problem,' the waitress said. 'How about you? Did you enjoy the breadsticks?'

'Aye, they're good,' I said. 'Very nice. I'm probably a bit less mental about them than the wife, but very tasty all the same.'

The waitress nodded. 'She's a character,' she said.

'She is that,' I agreed.

I left her a handsome tip to offset the cost of any future counselling that might be required, then – pizza box in hand – I went outside and stood on the pavement, bewildered.

5

Retail therapy – I decided that would be the most effective way to calm my beans about Wilma's jitters. I'd considered hitting the Horseshoe Bar, but there was the potential for that to go either way. On the one hand, it might very well have had the desired effect and made me forget all about my troubles. But there was also the possibility that a few drinks could focus my thinking even more strongly on the wedding getting cancelled.

It's a delicate balance – no doubt all down to sensitive chemical reactions and what not. Far too risky at this particular juncture.

So retail therapy it was. Within a few minutes of leaving the restaurant I was standing in front of the shop window on Buchanan Street again, pizza box tucked safely under my arm, transfixed.

The longer I stood there staring at the thing – no doubt looking a bit demented to your average passer-by, with my mouth hanging open and my palms all sweaty – the more I came to believe that if I just went for it and bought the suit, then the wedding would *have* to go ahead. It's hard to explain the logic behind it – probably cause it's totally fucking illogical – but it seemed to make sense to me at the time. If I had a suit for the wedding, then how could there be no wedding? Particularly if the suit in question was *that* suit. There would have to be a wedding, otherwise what was the point of there being a suit for the wedding?

You see the level of derangement I'd reached by the time I finally wandered into the shop?

Pretty spectacular.

But there you go, that's the mindset we're dealing with.

I got myself in a right flap trying to find the thing on the racks once I got inside as well. A panic attack, I suppose you'd call it. Shortness of breath, palpitations, bright flashing lights obscuring my vision. I dropped the pizza box at one point, and just about ended myself as it fell onto the floor beside me, forgetting I'd even been holding it.

'Can I help you with anything, sir?' an assistant asked me while I was kneeling down on the floor, closing the box up again, and I treated him a bit like I'd have treated a Saint Bernard coming out of the mist if I'd been stranded on a snow-covered mountain.

'Aye,' I said, tucking the box back under my arm and getting to my feet. 'Aye, you certainly can, son. I'm having a hell of a time here. I'm trying to find that suit you've got in the window. I came in and tried it on earlier, but I can't find it for the life of me now.'

He looked me up and down and came to the conclusion that my current outfit met with his approval, despite the pizza – as well it might.

He spoke to me in something not much louder than a whisper. 'We've moved those into the back, sir. Too many fly-by-nights roughing them up with grubby fingers. What size are you looking for? Forty-inch chest? Thirty-three-inch inside leg?'

I gave him the exact statistics and he nodded appreciatively, with his eyes closed.

'Just give me a minute,' he said. 'I'll be right back. Have a look at our new line in shirts while you're waiting.'

So I did just that.

He took his time coming back, the boy. I'd had a good mooch about amongst the shirts, deciding I might as well treat myself to one of them into the bargain. Then I'd started rummaging amongst the suits they had out on the peg, with a vague promise to myself that if I could find anything substantially cheaper than the one in the window I'd at least consider trying it on. There was a brown and yellow thing that was passable, and as I pulled it out to have a proper look, the edge of the hanger whacked somebody standing next to me, and before I could even turn to apologise he was saying, 'Now, you're a man who knows a thing or two about haute couture. Maybe you could help me out. How do you think this one would look on me?'

And when I turned and clocked the guy – fully registered who it was I was dealing with – I have to admit I felt more than a tad miffed. Are you ready for this? Can you believe whose potato-like face I was staring into? Eh? Fucking McFadgen. The brave detective. As bold as brass, holding up what looked like a bowling club blazer – navy blue with a daft wee crest on the breast pocket – smiling at me for all the world as if we were the best of pals.

'Aww, for fuck's sake, Duncan,' I said. 'Come on, gie's peace, pal. I'm busy here. This is serious business, McFadgen.'

But he just kept offering me the cheesy grin. 'Small world, eh?'

'Suspiciously small,' I told him. 'What are you after this time? Come on. This constant surveillance is getting to be beyond a joke.'

'This is purely a coincidence,' he said. 'Honest to God. I'm just in looking for something to wear to the police social.'

'The what?'

'The police social.'

'What in the name of fuck is that?' I said. 'Police social? That's the first time I ever heard those two words in the same sentence, let alone jammed up against one another. What the fuck is a police social?'

'A wee party. A dinner dance-type thing. They happen

about every six months. I'd just as soon give it a miss, but Liz loves them. So I'm trying to find myself something to wear.'

'In here? Is this a regular supplier of the McFadgen wardrobe?'

He shook his head. 'First time in,' he said.

'I'll bloody bet it is,' I said. 'You're full of shit, McFadgen. But fair enough, let's see it. What is it you're considering?'

He held the blazer up in front of him again. 'To be perfectly honest, I'm feeling quite intimidated in here. How does this look? Is it me?'

'This event,' I said, 'this fictional social . . . whatever you're calling it . . . is it fancy dress?'

'Eh?'

'Is there a theme? Pimps and prostitutes? Something like that?'

'It's a dinner dance, I told you. Smart evening wear.'

'Right,' I said. 'Then, naw, it doesn't look right. If there was some kind of mad theme, then maybe. But otherwise . . . here, sling me that and I'll pick you out a couple of alternatives.'

It was a stick-on that the whole thing was a set-up. He was in there to start badgering me about Dougie Dowds again – there was no doubt in my mind about that. But I had the idea that if I sent him into the dressing room with a couple of jerkins I could maybe give him the slip. So I picked out a couple of the most inappropriate jackets I could find and handed him them.

'Away and try these,' I said. 'That's closer to the sort of thing you're needing with a build like yours. And your unique complexion. There's the changing rooms behind the shoes there. Away and see if they fit.'

But he was like a fucking limpet. 'There's a mirror here,' he said. 'I hate changing rooms, they're too claustrophobic. Hang on to my coat, I'll just fire them on here.'

It's a wonder the staff hadn't already turfed him out onto the pavement, the nick of the gear he was wearing. The coat he handed me could very well have come out of the station archives, removed at some point in the past from a particularly grotty flasher they'd busted in Maxwell Park. Mind you, it turned out the coat had been performing an admirable public duty by shielding the world from the suit that lay beneath it. Have supermarkets started selling suits now as well? I know they've been stocking shitey pyjamas and T-shirts, fleeces and tracky bottoms for a while now, but this number McFadgen was sporting strongly suggested that one of the lower-end hypermarkets must have decided to expand its range into office wear on top of everything else.

'Jesus Christ . . .' I muttered when I clapped eyes on it. It was an involuntary reflex – my aesthetic sensibilities deeply offended on a purely instinctual level.

He peeled off the suit jacket and handed me that as well. There were big sweat stains under the oxters and I quickly dropped it onto the pole that the blazers were hanging on.

And then, to my great relief, the boy appeared from the back room with the suit he'd gone to get me, and he marched up to liberate me from the distressing experience of watching McFadgen trying to wiggle his way into the purple blazer I'd set him up with.

'There's a slight problem,' the boy said. 'We sold the one in your size about half an hour ago. I can reorder it, but I've brought you one that's slighter smaller and one that's slightly larger, just to try. Sometimes you find the sizes aren't completely standardised anyway, so you might be in luck. Are you happy to try these?'

I wasn't for hanging about. 'Aye, I'll take a crack at it, son. No problem.'

I grabbed the merchandise and legged it towards the changing rooms, leaving McFadgen grunting and wheezing behind me, getting himself into a right fankle as he tried to wrestle his flappy shirt into the sleeves of the jerkin.

'Is there something I can help you with there, sir?' I heard the boy asking him as I made good my escape. 'That's a lovely jacket, but you might just need to try it in a slightly broader fitting.'

There's something ritualistic about stepping into a quiet cubicle in changing rooms and pulling the curtain shut behind you. It's calming. You're all set to re-upholster yourself, try out a new skin. You've got the item in question hung up on the convenient hook, you're sitting on the wee bench untying your shoelaces, and you just think to yourself, here we go – fired up to see how this particular item's going to look on you.

Few moments in life are quite as pleasurable. It's like a place of sanctuary in there, an oasis of peace in a world gone mad. Especially, I find, when there's a homicide detective on the other side of the changing-room wall, fully intent on asking you some pretty awkward questions – no matter how much he might be trying to convince you he's just bumped into you by accident.

With the shoes off, I took a right good look at the suits the boy had given me, delighted to be seeing them up close again. I ran my fingers across the material to feel the quality, and then just stood there more or less awed at the beauty of the objects. The lining was something else altogether. It had a purple tinge to it, but only when the light caught it, and the stitching in there had been done in an orange thread. Fucking amazing. The pattern on the material itself was spectacular, leafs and branches, and as I looked at it closer, even the odd bird hidden here and there.

I gave some thought as to whether I'd try the larger or the smaller suit first, and in the end I plonked for the bigger of the two. More of a chance it would just be a no-no, and I wanted to save the more likely contender for last.

I'd just removed my trousers and started wrestling the replacements off the hanger, though, when there was a clinking noise on my left-hand side, and my protective curtain flew open.

'How does it look?' a voice asked, and I turned round expecting to see the boy from the shop floor, playing his hand too soon.

It happens.

Overenthusiasm.

Sometimes I even think they pull the stunt deliberately in the expensive places, just to check you're not stuffing any of the merchandise into your rucksack, ready to make a quick escape.

But as it turned out, it wasn't the boy at all. Not by a long shot. It was fucking McFadgen – posing in a blazer that looked like a flotation device on him while I stood there in my Y-fronts, exposed to the world.

'What do you think?' he said, swinging himself from side to side, presumably so's I could get a vague view of the jacket from a wheen of ever-so-slightly-different angles.

'About what, McFadgen?' I said. 'About the constant police harassment and invasion of my privacy? I'll be perfectly honest with you, pal. It's beginning to wear a bit thin.'

'About the *jacket*,' he said. 'The assistant recommended this one, but I'm swithering. I told him I'd get your opinion.'

'McFadgen,' I said, 'I'm standing here in my scants. Come back in ten minutes. You're a never-ending nightmare.'

I threw the curtain shut, and started pulling the suit trousers on, but McFadgen wasn't for moving.

'You got a good enough glimpse of it anyway,' he said.

'What's your opinion based on first impressions? Is it a goer?'

'I think the assistant's taking the piss,' I said. 'The same as you're taking the piss trying to pretend you're in here to shop. I know it's a crock, and the boy knows it's a crock. So he's taking you for a ride.'

The suit trousers were a touch baggy at the crotch. The extra length I could live with, it was easy enough to get that taken up. But the roominess in the groin area was a no go. Everything was flapping about. I made a grab for the jacket anyway, just in case it might sit better.

'I'll wait out here till you're finished,' McFadgen shouted, even though there was only a square of curtain between us. 'Maybe there's something else you can pick out for me. Take your time. I'll wait in this cubicle across the way.'

The jacket was better than the trousers, but still baggy. It gave me a fair idea of how I would look in a properly fitting one, though, and the prognosis was positive. They were my colours, no doubt about that. It was a hell of a look. Majestic, you might say.

'Listen, McFadgen,' I said, 'this is serious business for me. I'm a connoisseur of this stuff, and I need peace and quiet to get it done properly. Away out into the main body of the kirk and I'll see you when I'm done. You're hampering my critical faculties, sitting in there like a big lummox.'

'No problem,' he said, and I heard the bench creaking

as his ample weight eased up off it. He stepped out of his cubicle, but then he stopped. 'Oh, by the way,' he said, 'there's been a bit of a development in the Dougie Dowds case – we've made some further progress. A minor breakthrough, I think.'

'You don't say,' I muttered. 'That's the last thing I'd be expecting on the back of you turning up in here. On you go then, hit me with it. What's the latest revelation?'

And just as I dropped my kecks to try on the next suit he pulled the curtain open again.

'Aww, for Christ's sake,' I said. 'This is getting beyond a joke, pal. Is there something you like about seeing me standing here in my jockeys?'

'Not exactly,' he said. 'But I *do* like to see you standing in that confined space, Johnson – reminds me of something. Or maybe it's a vision of the future, rather than a memory. It's deeply pleasing anyway. It makes something sing deep down in my soul.'

We were getting to the nub of the matter now. I pulled the roomy trousers back up and sat down on the bench.

'Tell me this,' he said, leaning in towards me. I had an inkling he was attempting to look menacing, but the fact that he was standing there to all intents and purposes in a buoyancy aid spoiled the effect somewhat. Nevertheless, he stuck with it.

'Where were you on the afternoon of the nineteenth of June?' he said. 'Between the hours of two and three p.m.?'

'How in the name of Christ would I know?' I said. 'What day was that?'

'Scratch it,' he said. 'Let's try a different approach. How about the night before last, between nine and eleven – where were you then?'

'Probably in the living room,' I said, 'watching the telly.'

'Can anybody back that up?'

I gave it some thought. 'The wife was at her sister's, so it was just me. On my tod.'

'Exactly,' the wise one retorted.

I started to feel a bit dizzy. 'What are you talking about?' I said. 'What's supposed to have happened the night before last?'

He elbowed his way deeper into my cubicle and crushed up against the suit I had hanging on the hook.

'Nothing,' he said. 'Sweet F.A. And that's precisely my point.'

This was all starting to get a bit too much for me. All I wanted to do was try that second suit on and see if it was too tight or just right. I leant forward, put my elbows on my knees and my head in my hands.

'You're driving me daft, McFadgen,' I said. 'What the hell are you playing at here?'

'I'm showing you how things function in the everyday world, Johnson. That's all. You take any random human and you ask them where they were and what they were doing at any particular time on any particular day. There are two general outcomes. One, they can't remember. Or two, nobody can corroborate their story. The instances where somebody knows exactly where they were in a particularly narrow time frame, and that they've got a whole squad of witnesses to back them up, are exceptionally rare. That's just a fact of life.'

'It sounds like a lot of shite to me,' I said. 'How can that be right?'

McFadgen shrugged. 'Where were you on Wednesday last week? Say, between three and four?'

I gave it some serious thought this time. Wednesday night I was at Jinky's place; before that I'd had a fish supper with the wife. I worked my way back.

'I was driving up to Largs to pick up a delivery for John Jack,' I said.

'So you were in the car.'

'Bingo.'

'With who?'

I got his point. It was just me. Still, I was pretty certain he'd just hit a lucky instance.

'So here's what I'm thinking,' he said. 'How is it, with that being the case, with you being unable to remember or prove where you were for the vast majority of dates and times I might care to mention – how is it that for the very moment when Dougie Dowds was killed you can prove exactly where you were, without a shadow of a doubt, and with witnesses and corroborators up the yin yang? Does that not seem like a bit of an unlikely coincidence to you?'

I shrugged. 'A happy coincidence,' I said. 'What of it?'

'I'll tell you what of it, Johnson,' he said. 'I'll tell you right now.'

But he never, cause right at that minute the boy from the front of the shop appeared, calling out 'Hellooo' as he sauntered down the aisle, stopping now and again to pop his head into various cubicles.

'Up here, son,' I shouted, and when he reached us he lifted his eyebrows to see McFadgen stuffed into the wee box alongside me, trussed up in his life preserver. Still, give the boy his due, he took it in his stride as if it was the sort of thing that happened every day, and moved past it to ask me how I was getting on.

'This one's a bit roomy,' I said, standing up. I gave the material a tug at the front to show him what I was talking about, and he signalled his agreement.

'I've still to try the second one,' I said. 'The detective inspector here stopped in for a quick natter mid-session.'

'No hurry,' the boy said, still doing an admirable job of suggesting this was all completely normal. 'Just give me a shout if you need anything else. I'll be right outside. How about the blazer, sir?' He turned to McFadgen. 'Any decision on that yet?'

'I'm still getting Mr Johnson's opinion,' McFadgen said. 'I think we're leaning towards a no, but I'll keep you informed.'

'Very good,' the boy said, and he wandered off.

Since I was already standing up I took the opportunity to nudge McFadgen back out beyond the confines of the cubicle.

'Let me get at that other suit,' I said. 'Do you think we're about done here?'

He laughed. 'Far from it. We're only just getting started. And I'll tell you why. I've known from the get-go it was you that killed Dougie Dowds. And it's that alibi of yours that's always been the deciding factor – it's too neat. It's absolutely watertight, and that's always a red flag, in my experience. I told you the other night I was determined to crack it. I'm like a dog with a bone, Johnson – I'll stay with that type of thing until I can smash it to smithereens. Night and day. However long it takes me. I'll stick at it till it's done.'

'Aye,' I said. 'Well, good luck with that, McFadgen. All the best to you, pal.'

I started buttoning up the second jacket and it was clear from the off that it was going to be too tight. I sucked my belly in to get the buttons done up, but I was kidding myself.

'Oh,' McFadgen said, 'I don't need any luck. Not in the least. I told you already, we've had a new breakthrough in the case. There's been a further development. What did you think I was talking about all this time?'

I gave up on the jacket and peeled it off with a sense of sadness about the whole enterprise. Buying on impulse – that's what you often need to get you over the line when it comes to a purchase in that price bracket. I had the feeling that waiting for the boy to order the suit in my size would lead to a cooler head prevailing. And I hung the jacket back on the hook with a certain sense of defeat.

'I'll be perfectly honest with you, McFadgen,' I said. 'I've rarely got a Scooby Doo what you're talking about at the best of times, and as far as this afternoon's concerned, I've been totally in the dark. So hit me with it, what's this development you're banging on about? What have you discovered?'

'It's not so much a question of what we've discovered,' he said. 'It's more something we'd overlooked. Beforehand. Dougie Dowds died some time between ten to eight and twenty-five past, that's the template we've been working with. That was based on the fact that his body was found by a neighbour at twenty-five past eight, and that he texted me to rearrange our meeting just before ten to. So it stood to reason he died some time between ten to eight and twenty-five past. But then we realised what we'd overlooked.'

He paused and stared at me, and I got the feeling he was waiting for a response. He was a good deal more interested than I was in any of this, but I humoured him – just to try and put an end to it all.

'What's that?' I said.

'His phone,' McFadgen answered. 'It's slowly emerged that we don't actually have his phone. I've got his text on my phone, and we've got the record from the network proving the message came from his phone. But we don't actually *have* his phone. It's gone AWOL. Which, potentially, alters the estimation of the time of death considerably. If somebody else had his phone, and sent me that text at ten to eight, say from, oh, I don't know, say from somewhere like Rogano's, while they were out celebrating their anniversary, that would mean Dougie could already have been dead for an hour at that point. Maybe even two. Which, correct me if I'm wrong, leaves you high and dry without an alibi for the actual time of his death. Am I right?'

This didn't look great. Not so far as getting McFadgen off my tail was concerned. But I carried on with my business as if it was neither here nor there, dropping the baggy pants and stepping out of them, before I reached out for my own trousers hanging on the hook.

'I don't suppose you'll mind me asking where you happened to be at, say, seven o'clock on that night, Peacock. Or maybe even six? Have you got anything quite as solid for that time frame?'

I thought about it for a minute. 'I'd have to get back to you on that, Duncan. I'd probably have to check my diary. But here's the thing – it's all totally academic anyway. In fact, what you should do is pull out your own diary and we'll make ourselves a date for tomorrow, say for four o'clock in the afternoon, if you're free. Cause here's the thing – I didn't actually steal that painting from Pollok House.

In fact, I had absolutely nothing to do with it. But I've been to see John Jack, and John Jack's doing a spot of research into the question of who did nick it, right at this very minute. So if you want to set something up for tomorrow, I'll gladly pass that info on to you. And then we can call a halt to this constant harassment you're indulging in because you happened to read a bit too much into a daft book by Ian Rankin.'

I pulled up my Versace jeans, stuck my feet into my shoes, and sat back down on the bench to lace them up. But despite my heartfelt pitch, McFadgen seemed unmoved. He footered about inside the life jacket for a minute till he located something in his shirt pocket, and he pulled it out – a folded piece of paper.

'Nice try,' he said, 'but we're beyond that now. Way beyond that. You see this?'

He waved the paper about a bit, and then tapped it on the side of the cubicle. 'You know what this is?' he asked.

I gave it some thought. 'Your certificate for winning Fanny of the Year?'

'You wish,' he said. 'And well you might, cause if it was – it would mean a sight less trouble for you, Johnson. But unfortunately, what this is' – he gave it the wee tap on the cubicle wall again – 'is a warrant. A search warrant giving me the authority to search your flat. With the express intention of finding Dougie Dowds' mobile phone.'

He shook the paper till it unfolded and took a good look

at it. 'Two Regent Park Square, flat number five – that's you, right?'

I nodded.

'Then we're all set,' he said. 'I was round there earlier this morning – ready to get going. No answer. The boys were keen to knock the door in, but I convinced them to hold off. Makes a hell of a mess. I didn't like the thought of your wife having to deal with that, while you were sitting cooped up in your cell.'

'You're all heart,' I told him.

'So I checked the bookies. Then the Horseshoe. Nothing doing, so I knew you had to be in one of these places.'

'I take it that means you'll not be buying the jerkin,' I said. 'I knew that was a lot of shite.'

He leaned into the cubicle and took a good look at himself in the mirror. 'I think I'll go for it anyway,' he said. 'The police social's for real. Normally I'd go to Slater's, but this'll do me as well as anything else. Come on, let's go.'

I left the suits hanging in there for the boy to collect, and out on the shop floor McFadgen asked him to bag up the life jacket, and pulled his manky flasher's mac back on again.

'How about you, sir?' the boy asked me. 'Do you want me to order that suit in your own size? It should only take a couple of days.'

'Let me think about it,' I told him. For the time being, it had served its purpose in taking my mind off the bombshell the wife had dropped, back at lunch. And McFadgen's nonsense had continued to absorb me enough to make the bride-to-be's jitters seem like small potatoes. 'I'll drop back in before the week's end and let you know.'

And when McFadgen had paid up, we wandered out onto the street like a couple of pals.

'So how do you want to play this?' he asked me. 'Do I give you a lift to your flat and you give me easy access, or do we do it the hard way, with the battering rams?'

'Lead on, Sherlock,' I said. 'Here's the keys right here. And give me a proper look at that warrant just so's I can make sure we're all legal and above board.'

6

I left my flat the next morning with a real spring in my step. I was on my way to get the lowdown from John Jack, the sun was shining, and to top it all off, things had gone well for the wife the previous evening regarding her meeting with the nervous bride.

Or maybe that's not quite the right way of putting it. What I mean is, things had gone well for *me* the previous evening regarding the wife's meeting with the nervous bride. If I'm being perfectly honest about it, the wife had been none too chuffed with the outcome, or let's just say her reaction had been ambivalent at best.

'Well, that's me stuck looking like a mangled cupcake in public,' she said, when she clattered back into the flat about ten minutes past midnight, a touch the worse for wear.

'You managed to talk her into going through with it?' I said, trying my level best to keep my excitement under control.

'More fool me,' she said. 'Pour me a gin, Peacock. It's true what they say – no good deed goes unpunished. I can't believe I blew my chance to avoid wearing that monstrosity.'

She didn't have to ask me twice to pour her that drink. And I poured myself a good-sized one into the bargain. I was over the moon.

'What the hell happened here?' she said as she sat down and looked round about herself. 'Jesus Christ, Peacock, the place looks as if a bomb's hit it. Is this what happens when I go out for five minutes? What the hell have you been playing at?'

I handed her her drink with a paper umbrella in it, just the way she likes it.

'I'm in the process of tidying the place up,' I said. 'We've had another visit from Duncan McFadgen and a few of his pals. They claimed they'd find some kind of contraband goods if they tore the place apart, so that's exactly what they did. Big style.'

'In the name of God,' Bev said. 'How can they just go and leave the place like this? It's a total pigsty.'

Then the full import of what I'd just said began to sink in, and she started eyeing me up suspiciously. 'What have you been up to, Peacock? What were they looking for? I'm warning you – I told you if you started into anything dodgy again that would be it between you and me. And I meant it. Come on, what were they looking for?'

I shrugged my shoulders. 'Christ alone knows, hen.

McFadgen refused to tell me. It's a stitch-up. I'm clean as a whistle. Honest, Bev. It's still fallout from this Rankin book. I'm starting to think I should have sued the bastard for defamation when I had the chance.'

She looked at me and screwed her face up, then she started fiddling with her paper umbrella – disaster averted.

'They should at least be obliged to clean up after themselves,' she said. 'Coming into folks' homes. Is that not terrible?'

I managed to get the full story about Wilma's jitters out of her before we called it a night. It was your classic case of pre-match nerves, nothing more. Wilma had got it into her head that she hadn't known Vince long enough to fully get to grips with exactly who he was and what he was all about.

'I'm starting to think I might be rushing into this too quickly,' she'd told the wife. That seemed to be the general gist of it anyway. Apparently she'd started focusing on the details of Vince's backstory that were still a mystery to her, and imagining the worst to fill in the blanks.

The wife had hit her with a killer blow in the end.

'If everybody knew everything about their fiancé before the wedding took place,' she said, 'nobody would ever get married, Wilma. The human race would've died out before it even got started.'

Then she'd apparently spent some time drawing a comparison between the obvious attractions of the groom and my own particular shortcomings.

'That certainly put things in perspective for her,' Bev said. 'And I told her the best bit about marriage is the adventure of filling in all those blanks. God, I just about made myself boak. And now I'm consigned to wearing that bloody dress for my sins. I don't suppose McFadgen and his pals tore the dress apart, did they? Looking for drugs in the lining or something?'

But I had to tell her she'd had no such luck. They'd left it lying on the bed in more or less perfect order.

I suppose I have to give McFadgen credit for some of the spring in my step as I headed to J.J.'s as well, though. Just thinking about his mounting frustration the previous afternoon fair cheered me up.

He'd radioed ahead as he drove us to the flat, and there were a few of his goons waiting outside the door when we got there, just itching to get in about things.

McFadgen himself steered me straight through the hall and sat me down at the kitchen table, stationing one goon beside me with orders to keep me under strict surveillance, while the rest of them – McFadgen included – set about destroying the place in their hunt for Dougie Dowds' phone.

It was a good three hours they were at it. By the time McFadgen admitted defeat I'd just finished getting my guardian angel to heat up the eggless pizza in the oven for me, and the two of us were sitting wiring into it with a bottle of beer each.

'Help yourself,' I told McFadgen. 'You must be knackered, pal. Pull up a chair and join us.'

I suppose you'd have to use the word livid to describe his overriding emotional state. Or maybe fucking raging would be the more accurate term. Either way, he initially took it out on my bodyguard, telling him to piss off back to the station – where he'd already sent the other two empty-handed marauders. The boy at the table didn't have to be told twice. He grabbed the slice of pizza he was in the process of demolishing and legged it, and McFadgen just stood there with his back against the fridge, giving me the evil eye.

'That was a tad rude, Duncan,' I told him. 'Me and Scott there were on the verge of forming a beautiful new friendship. He seems like a good sort.'

'Shut up, Johnson,' he said. 'I'm at my limit. I'm this close to charging you with wasting police time.'

'How?'

'Cause you've wasted my whole afternoon. Three hours, and we've come up with nothing.'

'That's the customary result when you go chasing after rainbows, Duncan,' I said. 'You need to give yourself a break, pal. You'll end up demented.'

He pushed himself away from the fridge and lumbered his way towards the table, bending down to look into my face. 'I know you had that phone. And *you* know you had that phone. Whatever you did with it, I'll find out. And what's more, it'll be you that tells me – in the end. I'm going to grind you down, Johnson. All the way. I know it was you that did this, and I'll get you for it. You've got my word on that.'

I stood up. I'd had just about enough of him for the one day. 'Listen, McFadgen, I told you back in the shop, and I'm telling you again now, get your diary out. We're meeting up tomorrow afternoon, and I'm telling you who it was that stole that painting. And when I do, you're getting off my case. On top of ripping my house apart you've already seen me in my Y-fronts, and this is where the invasion of privacy ends. You're meeting me at four o'clock tomorrow afternoon, in the Horseshoe, and once you've got your information you're leaving me alone for the foreseeable future, or I start proceedings for harassment. Right?'

I even managed to persuade him to take a wee slice of pizza before he left, and I decided in the end that it was probably worth having the flat pillaged to within an inch of its life just to see him so properly wound up about having found sweet fuck all.

So, as I climbed up the stairs to John Jack's office, I doubt if I could have been feeling better – not without a drink in me anyway. Within a couple of hours I'd have the word on who had swiped that painting, and I'd have passed the intelligence on to the detective inspector, and on top of that, it was all systems go for Wilma's wedding. McFadgen would be off my tail, and I'd be entirely at liberty to lay the groundwork for my infallible money-making enterprise, in plenty of time to have it up and running the minute the minister had told Vince Cowie he may now kiss the bride.

Magnificent.

I gave J.J.'s door a good hard knock, and admired the sun shining in through the window at the end of the corridor – all set.

Whenever there's a darts tournament in progress, and you're obliged to have any kind of dealings with John Jack, you only ever end up thinking one thing: 'I wish to Christ there was a snooker tournament on instead.'

I mean, give him his due, he can still be a right grumpy bastard when the snooker's on as well. Especially if you interrupt his viewing at a crucial moment, or if the boy he's been touting for the match takes a beating. But it's a different thing with the darts – the outcome of the individual game is irrelevant, as is the stage of play you interrupt him at. The telly doesn't even need to be on when you visit him – he just gets himself into this *mood* for the duration of the competition. Het up, I suppose you'd call it. All aggro.

When it's the snooker that's on, barring the occasional upset, the game itself seems to have a calming effect on him. It'll oftentimes put him into a kind of meditative state while he's watching it, something almost trance-like. And that relaxed vibe'll be the underlying mode of his being for as long as the tournament lasts.

Relatively speaking, of course.

Granted, if you stood him next to your average yoga instructor or man of the cloth he'd still appear to be a raging volcano of unadulterated bile, but in comparison to his everyday self, there's a difference.

With the darts it goes the other way. I'm not even convinced that a man with his blood pressure should be indulging in watching the arrows. But be that as it may, he's a right nippy bastard from the opening throw to the lifting of the trophy at the end. And as soon as I stepped into his private domain, I was on the receiving end of it.

Or to be more specific, my latest money-making idea was on the receiving end of it.

'I'll tell you the main problem with this pie in the sky shite of yours,' he said, 'if you're looking for my advice.'

Note that this was before we'd even exchanged pleasantries. I was barely in the door. He was sitting at his desk, his wee telly broadcasting the opinions of a couple of pundits on the darts match that had just wound up, and he started unpeeling the wrapper from the body of a sausage-sized cigar.

'And a good morning to you too, John,' I said. 'How are you keeping?'

'DNA,' he said. 'That's your problem, right there.'

'DNA?'

'Exactly. Everything's DNA these days. That's the first-stop shop. The immediate go-to. They totally bypass finger-printing in the majority of cases nowadays. Go straight for the DNA. So if you're looking for the answer to the problem with your latest idea, that's it right there – DNA.'

I walked up to his desk and leant myself against it. 'What gave you the notion I was looking for an answer to any problems with my idea?' I asked him. 'The thing's a belter, John. Ironclad. This is the big one. Guaranteed.'

'You're living in the nineteenth century,' he said. 'What the fuck do you think this is, Peacock? Victorian London? Some clown with a pipe and a magnifying glass? You're doomed to an embarrassing failure. Yet again.'

'Tell me this, John,' I said. 'When does the next snooker championship kick off? Anytime soon?'

'Eh?'

'When do the darts finish? When's the next battle of the green baize?'

He frowned at me and fished out a pocket diary. I'd had the idea that if it was only a couple of days away I might just come back later, rather than stand there soaking up all his snash. I mean, my idea was big enough and bold enough to take the battering, but he was starting to take the edge off the bright mood I'd been luxuriating in ever since I left the flat.

As it turned out, though, it was another week and a half until the darts came to a halt, and a full fortnight until the snooker got going, so I sucked it up and resigned myself to brazening it out.

'Let's leave your analysis of the contemporary methods of forensic detection to one side for the minute, John,' I said. 'You know what I'm here for. I'm looking for the lowdown on that painting. What's the story? Any joy?'

'Ha!' he said. Not a laugh or anything, just a brusque ejaculation of that solitary word. 'You don't want to know, Peacock,' he went on. 'Forget that. It's a no go.'

'You got nothing?'

'On the contrary. *I* know exactly who it was. That's not what I'm saying. I'm saying *you* don't want to know. Forget it. Let it go.'

'What for?'

'Just take my advice. Walk away. Forget you ever asked.'

'You're refusing to tell me?'

'That's about the size of it. And like I said, it's in your best interests.'

Are you starting to see what I mean about the darts here? Just pure contrariness, no two ways about it. And I'll tell you what else, when he gets into a state like that, there's no arguing him out of it. It's just a constant stream of patronising bullshit: 'This is what's wrong with your business venture', 'This is what it's best you don't know'.

Horse shit.

But luckily, I'm a man with a plan. I never have to wait long until a zinger comes along to point me in the right direction. And that was as true on this occasion as it is on any other. As soon as my initial rush of frustration eased off, and I'd fought the urge just to kill the big fat bastard, there was a cracking solution already sitting there, right in the front of my brain. The old Johnson synapses very rarely let me down.

The move involved three stages.

Stage one.

'Have you heard about the latest development regarding Dougie Dowds?' I said. 'The bold McFadgen's had a bit of a breakthrough.'

He fair changed his tune at that. The darts adrenaline took a backseat to his information addiction. The eyes popped, and he very near tried to climb his way across the desk.

'Should I take that as a no?' I said.

'What's happened?' he asked me, and I told him to get his journal out of the desk drawer. He went about the task in something of a fury.

'If I tell you this,' I said, 'I want the info on that painting. No ifs or buts. Right? Regardless of whether you think it's in my best interests or otherwise.'

He nodded furiously. I knew there was no question of me getting the word on the painting before I'd delivered the goods. Right at that minute, he'd have been unable to access the information even if his life depended on it. He was consumed by his need to know what I was about to tell him, switched to input mode only. The rest of his mental apparatus had completely shut down. Clearly, the risk was he'd rescind on his end of the bargain once he'd got what he wanted from me, but that's where the second and third stages of my plan came in, so I'd no other option but to take the risk and just go for it.

'The estimated time of death's been extended,' I said. And then I laid out what McFadgen had told me about the methods that had been used to first fix it, and the fact that they'd overlooked his missing phone.

'This is gold dust,' the big fella muttered to himself, and he did everything in his power to set the paper in his jotters on fire, writing at the speed of I don't know what. He was like a man on the first rush of a highly powerful drug, getting his fix of the thing that gripped him to the core of his being.

'Here's the good bit, though,' I said, and he stopped abruptly and stared at me with the pupils dilating ever further, unable to believe there was more to come. 'McFadgen's got it into his nut that whoever sent that text on Dougie's behalf is still in possession of the phone, and all he has to do is get his mitts on the phone to prove who the murderer is.'

A big belly laugh erupted from the far side of the table, and after blackening a couple more pages with copious notes, J.J. threw himself back in his sturdy leather chair – spent, you might say. And he slowly closed his book and relit his cigar.

'So McFadgen reckons you've got this phone tucked away

somewhere?' he asked me, and I confirmed the deduction. And I moved my troops into position to commence the launch of stage two.

'He ripped the shit out of the flat yesterday,' I said. 'Destroyed the place.'

'Without a warrant?'

I shook my head. 'Wired to the teeth. All the relevant paperwork in order and a team in uniform to help perform the carnage.'

'That's a fucking liberty,' he said, and I breathed a sigh of relief, grateful that my gambit had paid off. 'This is the kind of thing that gets me fuming, Peacock,' he continued. 'The persecution our community endures at the hands of these jumped-up busybodies is beyond a joke. And what recourse have we got? Fucking none. I take it they never even cleared up behind themselves?'

'Not as much as a sock,' I said, and let him carry on for a good ten minutes, uninterrupted.

'The community' he was referring to, by the way, was the haphazard collection of thieves, loan sharks, drug dealers and GBH merchants that he generally associates with on a daily basis. And it's a particular bugbear of his that the police are continuously trying to get in about us, pushing their allotted powers to the limits.

'Just about every other previously persecuted minority's asserted their rights,' he often says. 'It's time for us to stand up and do the same thing. It's gone on long enough.'

Somewhat misguided you might say, and you'd be right, but my thinking here – going into stage two – was that if I could get him to unleash his darts aggression on somebody other than myself, then it would leave the way clear for me to put the final stage of my scheme into operation without risking the possibility of him just reverting to our earlier dynamic, and having a go at me again. He'd be drained, you see? He'd have got it all out his system, and I'd be well on my way to getting the data I'd come for in the first place.

Pretty nifty, eh?

And so I moved on to the final stage, and the thinking was this. Rather than just ask him a direct question, I'd bum him up a bit. Get him to boast his way into revealing the intelligence. So off I went.

What you want to do with the Jackster in an instance like this is make him feel like he's some kind of genius, impressing you with the brilliance of his insights and the depths of his knowledge, which, if I have to be perfectly honest, isn't the easiest thing in the world. The guy's actual mental capabilities are so average to middling that you have to make yourself seem pretty much on the edge of brain damage to achieve the right effect, but needs must.

I took a deep breath and battered myself down to just about as stupid as I could get. 'Here's what I never understood about stealing a painting like that Pollok House one, John,' I said. 'I could never quite figure out what the fuck the point of it was. I mean, how on earth are you ever going to sell the thing? The whole world's on the lookout for it – it's hardly as if the numptie that buys it could ever display it. It seems to me it must be pretty much unsellable.'

He took the bait. He shook his head slowly as if I was a total eejit, and adopted the patronising tone of voice. 'I worry about you sometimes, Peacock,' he said. 'Nobody's nicking these things to sell them as paintings. Are you daft?'

And he gave me a slow lecture – as I pretended that I was finally seeing the light – about how these things are used as currency in the criminal underworld, as assets and standards to borrow against and used to set exchange rate mechanisms, much like gold in the slightly less shady economies. It was all standard stuff, but it did the trick, got him thinking he was a high priest and I was the impressed student, staring at him in awe as I learned at his knee.

'That's an eye-opener,' I said, when he'd reached his climax. 'I should get in on some of that myself sometime, John. It beats me how you know all that stuff. So how did you go about finding out who had whipped the painting? How would you even go about something like that?'

'It was simple,' he said. 'I just worked backwards.'

'From where?'

'From who it was that's got the painting at the minute.'

'But how do you even work something like that out?'

'I just put the word out that I was looking to buy it, and that I was wanting to find out how much the current holder was wanting for it. I claimed I was looking to do a cross-border deal where cash or precious stones would be too risky, and I was looking at the possibility of using the painting instead.'

I have to admit, I was actually quite impressed with this wee detail. I'm an ideas man – ideas appeal to me – and this particular one came across as elegant and simple. I didn't even have to *act* impressed at that one.

'So who had their mitts on it?' I asked him. 'Any word?'

'A guy called Stanley Frazer,' he said. 'He's mainly an importer. He bought it as a permanent asset he can borrow against in the future. Paid cash for it.'

Then he went into the whole history of how the painting had wound its way towards this Stanley Frazer character. How he'd bought it from another guy who had taken it as payment in a drugs deal with some guy called Chaz Anderson. It was clear Johnny Boy was getting a real buzz out of displaying his inside knowledge, much in the same way one of those nutters that collects Fabergé eggs or valuable old comics would get in a sweat laying out their prize possessions for you.

'Chaz Anderson's the real winner in this whole scenario,' he said. 'He probably paid about five hundred quid for the painting to be stolen in the first place – maybe a grand – and bought himself into business with it to the value of somewhere in the region of twenty grand, I'm guessing.'

He appeared to have reached the end of his narrative. I have to admit, I was wilting, but I put the bright face on it.

'You're some boy, John,' I said. 'Unbelievable. One of a kind, no question. So hit me with it, who's the mug this Chaz Anderson paid to do the dirty for him? Who's the genius behind the scenes with the sticky fingers?'

He sniffed. 'I told you before. You really don't want to know.'

'I'm aware of that,' I said. 'Painfully. But I've already given you that stash on McFadgen and his latest findings. You're owing me. It's up to me if I'm willing to take the risk of knowing who it was, surely? Who was the fall guy? Who slipped into Pollok House and did the deed?'

It was clear he was itching to finish his story, to get the full satisfaction of showing he'd really uncovered this whole thing. But he was still swithering. It was almost touching in a way, realising he wanted to protect me to the extent that he was willing to forgo a public display of his powers.

Then it got too much for him. 'Fuck it,' he said, and he told me.

He told me, and I realised immediately that he'd been right – absolutely right. I *really* didn't want to know.

I staggered back a bit, losing my balance a smidgeon. I found my way to the couch behind me and dropped myself down onto it, leaning forward and trying to focus on the manky brown carpet. I wondered if there'd been an earthquake, or something else that had tilted the room on its axis. Nothing seemed steady. Everything appeared to be squint.

I couldn't quite believe what he'd told me. I couldn't quite believe the name that he'd given me.

Are you ready for this?

Here we go: the chump who'd stolen the painting for Chaz Anderson, and who'd therefore whacked Dougie Dowds to stop him delivering the news to Duncan McFadgen, was none other than Vince Fucking Cowie – Wilma Caldwell's fiancé. The man my whole future fortune depended upon.

The shitting *groom*.

7

No doubt you're thinking to yourself at this juncture, 'What's this bampot's problem? How come he's getting himself tied up in knots about some random *wedding*? What's the story?'

And well you might – well you might.

I daresay I should probably have outlined the set-up a bit earlier on in the narrative, but I don't think you'll disagree that I've had my hands more or less full from the get-go with this, that and the other.

Still, there's no time like the present to make amends for past transgressions, so here we go. Here's the deal . . .

One night, maybe a couple of months ago, I'm sitting in the living room watching a documentary about an American conceptual artist. Strange choice, you might think, but I've got something of a soft spot for these conceptualists. For one thing, a fair few of them are from Scotland – and more often than not from Glasgow, if we're being specific. So there's a wee bit of hometown pride there. But that's only the half of it. Like I've probably mentioned once or twice already, I'm an ideas man myself, a boy for the brain flashes, and that's the same deal with these conceptualists. Idea merchants you might well call them. So I always get a buzz hearing about their work. Hearing the mad nutcase stuff they come up with.

Take that boy who turned the plinth upside down so that he could claim the planet itself was sitting on his plinth, and the whole world was his work of art – that kind of thing fair tickles me. Then you've got the other one turning up at the gallery to assemble his exhibition and he's brought nothing with him. So he has a look at the place, has a wee think, and then asks them to drill a few holes in the white walls. He sticks a fag through each hole, lights it up, and smokes it through the hole – leaving big burn marks on the white paint.

And that's his exhibition.

Totally magic.

And they pay these bods a fortune into the bargain. I tell you, that's the kind of ideas I wish I could have. Nine times out of ten the ideas that hit me are simply ideas for some crime or another, but if I could choose what type of ideas would come into my head, I'd much rather it was some of these art ideas.

Anyway, that's a pretty long road for a shortcut when all I'm really trying to say here is that I often watch these documentaries, trying to train myself to maybe have an idea like that sometime. And a couple of months ago I'm sitting watching this one about an American guy who makes these things using wood, just the same shapes over and over again, and at one point he's describing his process and he says something like, 'I use a very delicate sander, it's very slow and very subtle. It's the same machine criminals use for removing their fingerprints.'

And all of a sudden I'm like 'Woah. Hang on there just a minute'. And I rewind the box and listen again, and sure enough I'd heard him right the first time. And I'm thinking, 'Maybe in America, pal. I'll give you that. But as far as I'm aware I've never heard of anything like that over here. No way.'

And I ask a bunch of folk, and nobody I know's ever heard about it either. But I look into it properly, and sure enough – in certain places – it's a *thing*. And I realise that I've stumbled onto a goldmine.

It turns out it's a long slow procedure. You need to sit with your fingers being finely sanded by this thing for hours at a time, over multiple sessions. But to me that only makes it more perfect. You're going to be able to charge an hourly rate, which'll fair mount up over time. So I work out what I could charge per paw, multiply it by the endless supply of members from the 'community' that would do whatever it took to be free of their fingertips, and I realise that I'm home and dry. Minted.

The only drawback is the prohibitively expensive price tag on one of these machines, to which you'd need to add the price of safe premises to house the business, and no doubt a good whack of electricity to keep it up and running. So as you already know, I took the idea to John Jack. And as you also already know, he told me to stick the proposition up my proverbial.

Just bad timing, I suppose. His man was losing in the snooker at the time, and I was already quite deep in the hole with him, owing to a few recent projects that hadn't recouped their initial financial investment. Or that had gone tits up, to express it in the vernacular. But I suppose I have to thank his keenness to get rid of me for what happened next.

'Take it to Brian Caldwell,' he said. 'I hear he's about to come into some money.'

'How come?' I asked him.

'His ex-wife's about to get remarried. Brian's been making hefty alimony payments ever since the divorce. As soon as Wilma ties the knot, the agreement'll be null and void. He'll be rolling in it.'

Now, no doubt the Jackster thought Brian would be as keen to give me the bum's rush as he himself had been. Maybe he thought I wouldn't even bother going to see Brian, after the rubbishing he had just given the idea. But he was wrong. Seriously wrong. On both accounts. I went straight to see the Caldwell fellow, to congratulate him on his good fortune, and he in turn congratulated me on the spectacular potential of my idea, when I'd laid it out for him.

'How did John Jack find out about my situation, though?' he said. 'How did he find out I'm about to have some cash to spare?'

'You never told him yourself?'

'I hardly know John Jack,' he said. 'Our uncles are cousins – something like that. I rarely see the guy.'

I shook my head. Classic J.J.

Brian Caldwell himself isn't what the Jackster would call a member of the community. He's an architect by trade, strictly law-abiding. I know him from the days when he was married to Wilma, what with Bev being Wilma's best pal and what not. But the somewhat dodgy nature of the proposition I'd put to him didn't seem to be a problem. All that mattered to him was that it looked guaranteed to turn a healthy profit.

'Who knows if this wedding'll ever actually happen,' he said. 'It's a real on-again-off-again affair. As far as I hear, Wilma's constantly getting cold feet. But if it actually takes place, you can count me in, Peacock. The money'll just be burning a hole in my pocket otherwise.'

So over the next few weeks we firmed up the arrangement. Come the wedding, Brian would take out a loan to cover the capital investment in the sanding machine, and his recouped alimony would take care of the monthly payments on the loan, as well as the rent and rates for appropriate premises. He'd originally wanted a fifty per cent share of the profits in exchange for his investment, but I'd slowly ground him down – pointing out that I was bringing the customer base as well as the conceptual framework for the business, not to mention the fact that I'd have to perform whatever hard labour was involved in the day-to-day running of the operation.

After that, I'd just been counting the days, up until this very morning in John Jack's office when I'd sat with my head between my legs gasping for breath, sick to my stomach at the thought that I'd sent the whole thing up the spout. What a fucking situation. I'd told McFadgen I'd bring him a name to get him off my back, and now the name I was going to have to give him was the very name that would bring the whole enterprise crashing to the ground. Vince Cowie would be locked up for the murder of Dougie Dowds, the wedding would be cancelled, and the funds that were meant to catapult me into the world of the independently wealthy would continue, instead, to keep Wilma Caldwell in the style she'd grown accustomed to, out there in Bearsden.

'I told you you'd have been better not knowing,' John said as I lifted myself wearily off his couch and made my way towards the door.

'You certainly did,' I said. 'I can't argue with that, John. You were right on the money there.'

'If it's any consolation,' he said, 'your business idea was

doomed to failure anyway. DNA – that's what it's all about nowadays. Fingerprints are a thing of the past.'

'Cheers, pal,' I said. 'You're all heart.'

And I made my way down the stairs and out onto the street, slightly less affected by the brilliance of the sunshine than I'd been on my way in.

8

McFadgen was a good fifteen minutes late for our tête-à-tête. I'd found myself a seat up against the back wall of the café, ordered myself a roll and sausage and a pot of tea, and demolished the greater part of them both before he had the good grace to show himself.

By rights, I should have been using the extra time to work out what the fuck I was going to say to him, but before the waiter even dumped my order down on the table in front of me, I'd noticed that a few of McFadgen's pals were dotted about the place at tables on their own. Different numpties from the ones who'd helped him demolish my flat, granted, and dressed up to look like the average tool that would be sitting about on their tod in a café like this, at this time of day. But they were familiar faces to me. I'd seen them here and there over the years, in uniforms and in squad cars, throwing their weight about in a typical manner, and I couldn't for the life of me figure out what they were doing here.

They were all avoiding looking at each other, and they were all avoiding looking at me, but that only served to make their presence more obvious. And I suppose all my speculating about what the fuck they were up to kept the back bit of my brain fully occupied – cause absolutely nothing was delivered regarding what I was going to do about Vince Cowie when the detective inspector arrived.

Wandering about the town, after I'd left John Jack's office, I'd had the vague notion that as long as I could keep McFadgen in the dark about Vince till the wedding took place, I'd be home and dry. As long as Wilma and Vince tied the knot, Brian Caldwell's alimony obligation would be null and void, and I'd be up and running with my business. True, I'd probably have played a part in hooking my wife's best pal up with a murderer, but I suppose there are winners and losers in any business venture. And I could always give McFadgen a tip-off about Vince before the honeymoon took place, if my guilty conscience got the better of me.

If you looked at things optimistically, it was entirely possible that all Vince had done wrong was whip a painting to cover the expenses he was bound to accrue in starting up a new life. There was every possibility it was the Chaz Anderson guy he'd sold it to that had done for Dougie Dowds, or even one of the painting's later patrons, desperate to cover up whatever it was they'd used the painting to fund. When you really thought about it, all those guys had a lot more to lose than Vince if the painting got traced back to them. There was no point in me prematurely hanging Vince for the theft of a cart. Live and let live, that's always been my overriding philosophy.

So I was determined to keep McFadgen off Vince's trail as much as I was to get him off mine. I just, as yet, had no earthly idea how in hell I was going to achieve it.

Anyway, McFadgen eventually deigned to bless us with his presence. He stood jerking at the café door for a minute, getting redder and redder in the face each time he pulled it towards himself, until he finally twigged that it was a push job and put a smidgeon too much weight behind it and came tumbling inside at a run.

He looked a right mess. He was blissfully unaware of the fact that the one button he'd bothered to fasten on his suit jacket was coupled with the wrong buttonhole, and the suit itself was even more ill-fitting than the one he'd been wearing the day before. It seemed to be struggling to decide whether it was dark brown or dark blue, and whereas he could usually have passed for a bowling-club treasurer, he was getting into the area more commonly frequented by dim-witted local councillors this afternoon.

It fair affected my self-esteem to realise a guy as sartorially challenged as McFadgen was causing me any kind of intellectual difficulty at all. How could somebody as immaculately turned out as myself possibly be in an inferior position to this vandalised scarecrow? It hardly bore thinking about.

He clocked me early on, and made the same effort to avoid looking at his pals as they were making to avoid looking at each other. Then he just about deafened me scraping the chair opposite my own out from underneath the table, and sat down with a strange gloating grin on his face.

'Sorry I'm late,' he said. 'I got held up.'

'Not a problem,' I told him. 'Your pals kept me company.'

He frowned and turned to look behind him. 'What are you talking about? What pals? Are you on something, Johnson?'

'Fair enough,' I said. 'Christ knows what they're doing here, but fair enough. So, how did the wife like the blazer you bought yesterday? Was she a fan?'

His face fell somewhat. 'I'll have to take it back. She says it makes me look like somebody's shoved a bicycle pump up my arse and inflated me. She hated it.'

'She's probably got a point,' I said, and he shrugged and slowly let that weird gloating smile come back onto his face as he leant across the table towards me.

'You've made a big mistake showing up here this afternoon,' he said. 'By the time we're through here, I'll have your balls gripped so tightly in my fist you'll be singing "Pie Jesu" in a high soprano.'

'What can I bring you?' the waiter said quietly to McFadgen. He'd appeared at the side of the table without either of us noticing, and McFadgen straightened himself up with a jolt.

'Oh,' he said. 'Aye. Eh, hand me that menu, Peacock. Let me see.'

I told the boy to bring me another roll and sausage.

He nodded, and McFadgen pushed the laminated list of options back across the table.

'Just give me a black coffee,' he said. 'No sugar.'

The boy sniffed, and as he wandered off McFadgen made what he thought was an unnoticeable hand signal to his back-up, who clocked it with what they hoped were undetectable glances. Then we were back to McFadgen's leaning-across-the-table routine again.

'Right,' he said. 'Where were we?'

'Something about you fondling my ball sack,' I said, 'if I'm remembering right.'

He rapped his knuckles on the table a couple of times. 'That night you were out for dinner with your wife. I've twigged to what all that losing-your-wallet nonsense was about. You were drawing attention to yourself, making sure the staff remembered you were there – and at what time. It's amateur-hour stuff. You thought you were consolidating your alibi.'

'So what? What's that got to do with anything? I'm here to let you know who whipped that painting. After that, your conspiracy theories have got shag all to do with me – I'm off the hook.'

He raised his eyebrows. Pulled a weird face. To be perfectly honest with you, the guy looked certifiably unhinged.

'And that's exactly where you've put yourself in the shit,' he said. 'You've played right into my hands. Because the very fact that you've turned up here this afternoon, with that purpose in mind, proves that it could only have been you that stole it.'

I have to admit, if there was any logic whatsoever behind his statement, it completely escaped me. As far as I was concerned, he seemed to have finally driven himself daft with his obsession to get me behind bars. But I was only half paying attention to what he was saying anyway. I was mainly in a total panic wondering how to hold up my end of the bargain, with Vince Cowie's name being strictly off limits. I figured all I could do was play for time, hoping some bright moment of inspiration would materialise.

'What the hell are you talking about, McFadgen?' I said. 'Me turning up to tell you who stole a painting, out the goodness of my heart, proves that it was actually *me* that stole it? What are you on, man?'

He was already leaning so far across the table I hadn't thought it was possible for him to get any closer to me, but give the boy his due, he managed it. He came so close that our brows were just about touching. The edge of the table must have been fair cutting into his gut.

'On the twenty-third of June,' he said, 'Dougie Dowds was on his way to tell me who stole the painting, but he never made it. Somebody went to extreme lengths to make sure he never made it. Then, yesterday afternoon, you tell me you're going to meet me here to let me know who stole it. And I – you might be interested to hear – put the word out to that effect. I started a covert whispering campaign. My boys have got a whole network of contacts on your side of the fence, as you're no doubt aware. So we spread the word far and wide. And yet, here you sit, as right as rain. Not even a moustache hair out of place. You see what I'm saying?'

'Not exactly,' I said, still waiting on that brainflash to occur.

'If it wasn't you that took that painting,' he said, 'you'd have met the same fate as Dougie Dowds. It stands to reason. You'd never have made it here. Somebody would have whacked you. Ergo, you're busted.'

'And that's what your goons are here for?'

He shrugged. 'Maybe you'll try and make a run for it, or maybe I'll just need a hand to take you in. Either way.'

I leant back in my seat to get further away from his sweaty brow, and I gave his proposition some consideration.

'There's one possibility you've overlooked in your scenario,' I said eventually, 'an obvious loophole you've missed.'

'I don't think so.'

I nodded. 'What if this name I'm about to give you belongs to a pal of mine –a lifelong pal, close as you like. In that instance, they'd hardly be likely to kill me.'

The statement had only been a logical response to the

hypothesis he was proposing. Just something that occurred to me while I was trying to work out if there was any flaw in his reasoning. But as soon as I said it, the floodgates opened. The gridlock in my grey matter evaporated, and a great wave of neural activity burst out across my synapses. I was on it. I had my solution. Vince Cowie was off the hook.

It was just the simple act of thinking of my pals that had lit me up, so I had to hand it to McFadgen. Without his prompting, I might never have come up with my idea. McFadgen, alone, had shown me the way. The gorgeous moron.

But his gloating look was back again. It had flickered for a second when I'd first rebuffed his claims, but only momentarily.

'You'd never turn a pal in, though,' he said. 'So even that possibility fails to hold water.'

He was probably right, but he didn't have to know he was right – because the particular pal I had in mind was well out of harm's way. At the exact moment the painting had been stolen, he was soaking up the sun in Magaluf. And he'd been there for a full week before it was lifted, and for another full week after that. Christ knows what genetic inheritance had given him the constitution to survive a jaunt like that, but whatever it was, he had it. And even more conveniently, he was currently away for a few days with the Tartan Army to watch Scotland getting whipped in Malta, so it would take McFadgen those few days at least to work out he'd been given a bum steer, and by that time I was bound to have come up with a more coherent plan.

'Not if I was desperate to get revenge on somebody in particular,' I said. 'And besides, he only stole a painting. Your whole theory about the person who stole the painting being the same person who bumped Dougie Dowds is pure fantasy. So what's the worst that can happen to him? Just about enough for me to be satisfied I've got him back. Give or take six months to a year.'

McFadgen shook his head. 'You're havering,' he said. 'It was you that stole the painting. It's a stick-on.'

'Not according to John Jack,' I said, and that certainly ruffled his feathers. 'When has John Jack ever been wrong about something like this?'

Finally, he sat back in his seat. He put his hands on top of his head, fingers laced through their opposite numbers, and moved his scalp back and forward. At the same time, the waiter appeared with McFadgen's coffee and my roll and sausage and laid them down on the table. I kind of regretted getting the second roll now – you know thon way? You're well up for it when you've just finished the first one, but in the interim you've realised one was probably enough, and it's just a case of your eyes having been bigger than your belly?

'Let me know if you need anything else,' the boy said as he wandered away, and I opened up my roll and squeezed some brown sauce onto it anyway.

McFadgen took his hands down off his napper and pushed his coffee cup about the table. 'So who was it?' he said. 'Who's John Jack saying it was?'

'I'll tell you what, McFadgen,' I said. 'I've just realised you were quite willing for me to be killed just to try and prove one of your daft theories. Putting my name about like that was pretty much signing my death warrant if it hadn't been a pal of mine who stole the painting. Am I wrong? You were willing to see me in a body bag, weren't you?'

He'd a kind of sickly leer on his face as he picked up his coffee. 'I'd have felt a momentary pang of sadness if you'd been murdered,' he said. 'But I'd have been quite happy if somebody had badly fucked you up – kneecapped you or something like that.'

'In which case,' I said, 'I'm no longer feeling inclined to give you the name, Duncan. And you know John Jack's the last person in the world that'll tell you.'

That got him. That convinced him that what I had for him was gospel, and he suddenly wanted it badly.

'I was joking,' he said. 'Obviously. I was a hundred per cent certain you took that painting. So, as far as I was concerned, you'd be right as rain.'

I fought against my reluctance to down the second roll and sausage and got battered into it. To be entirely honest, once I'd started, it was perfectly pleasant. I wasn't really sure what all the fuss had been about.

'Nah,' I said. 'You've gone too far this time, McFadgen.

Harassment and invasion of privacy's one thing, putting me in mortal danger's something else altogether. You've blown it, son. Forget it.'

'All right,' he said. 'All right, I admit it. The story of me putting your name about was just a fairytale. Satisfied? It never happened. I was trying to force the issue.'

'Hand on heart?'

'Straight up.'

I'd had a suspicion that was probably the case, but it was a relief to have it confirmed. If it really was Chaz Anderson that had done for Dougie Dowds, and if he'd found out I was on my way to point McFadgen in his general direction, I could really have been in for a fair bit of bother.

'And look at it this way,' McFadgen said, 'with that being the case, which it is, if you don't give me a name now we'll be right back to square one. And I'll be all over you like a rash again. Night and day.'

I made like I was badly put out. 'Fair enough,' I said. 'You're a prick, but fair enough. John Jack says it was Gordon Jenkins that liberated the canvas. Wee Jinky.'

McFadgen looked beyond surprised. 'Jinky?' he said, and I nodded. 'Really? I thought the two of you were joined at the hip. That must have been quite a number he did on you, for you to be grassing him up.'

'Don't even get me started,' I said. 'My blood's boiling just thinking about the bastard.'

The inspector stuck out his bottom lip and nodded slowly. 'Understood,' he said. Then he appeared to suffer the onset of a melancholic turn of mood. He picked his coffee up and stared into it, and it took him a good while to whack up the motivation to swallow a few gulps.

'I'd better get out there and arrest him then,' he said, without much enthusiasm for the task. 'Where's the best place to find him, you reckon? His flat?'

I shrugged. 'Should be,' I said. 'Like I told you, we're somewhat estranged at the minute. I'm less than interested in his comings and goings.'

McFadgen tapped the table a few times with his middle finger and then he suddenly brightened. I had the idea there was maybe a bit too much caffeine in his drink – it was a hell of a brisk turnaround. He even took another gulp at the stuff, without any humming and hawing beforehand this time.

'Maybe you were right after all, Peacock,' he said. 'For once. Maybe it's me that's in the wrong this time. Maybe there really *is* no connection between the theft of that painting and Dougie Dowds' murder. I'm starting to come round to your way of thinking.'

I eyed him a touch suspiciously.

'Look at it this way,' he said. 'If I've been barking up the wrong tree, then the fact that Gordon Jenkins nabbed that painting doesn't necessarily mean that you never killed Dougie Dowds.'

I groaned. 'It does, however, mean that the only thing you've got against me is the fact that I've got an alibi for the time it happened,' I said. 'That's your whack.'

'Exactly,' he said. 'I've still got that. As well as the probability that you sent me a text from Dougie Dowds' phone earlier in the evening.'

'Dream on,' I said.

But it seemed to be enough to lift him out of his crushing despair and get him up onto his feet. You can hardly begrudge a man that, I suppose.

He fished out a wallet and put a tenner down on the table. 'Pay the bill with that,' he said. 'I'll away and have a word with your Jinky, if I can find him. Then we'll get back to the business of trying to put you in Barlinnie.'

'If I as much as catch sight of you during the next fortnight I'll be filing that complaint for harassment, McFadgen,' I said. 'I've done you a big favour here, getting you that data from John Jack. Keep up your end of the bargain.'

He smiled – with the mouth, not with the eyes. 'We'll see,' he said, and he turned round and gave the nod to his goons, who exchanged puzzled looks with each other. For a minute, they seemed at a loss as to what to do, then one of them got up and followed behind McFadgen at a distance as he made for the door. I gave the other two a wee wave, and they got up and followed in turn, befuddled chumps looking to each other for some kind of explanation.

'What's happening?' one of them shouted after the bold detective, and then all four of them were gone.

I sat on with the remains of my second roll and sausage. I was pretty confident McFadgen would be off my tail for a good few days now. Trying to locate the Jinkster without knowing he was tucked away in Malta would keep him fully occupied, and his crack about me still being in the frame for the Dougie Dowds affair was strictly for his own benefit, to ward off the crushing depression brought on by his failure to get me into the jail again.

Still, it was clear that I wouldn't be using the breathing space to start getting the fingerprint business ready to go: what really mattered was making sure Vince Cowie didn't end up behind bars before he'd made his lifelong commitment to Wilma Caldwell. And that would need to be my prime objective for the foreseeable future. Setting up premises and everything else would just have to wait. Otherwise there'd be no fucking business to set up.

9

The eastern mystics talk a lot about the advantages of a totally empty mind. I watched a documentary about that on the telly one night, amid the chaos of Bev hammering on about some bampot in her work who was planning to buy a caravan or something – and how the bampot's husband was up in arms about it cause he hates having to shit in campsite toilets.

Something like that.

It made it a tad difficult to concentrate properly on the finer points of this documentary, but the general idea seemed to be that you have to remove as many distracting thoughts from your brain as you can before you're able to see things clearly. There was a boy in it who lived up at the top of a mountain somewhere or other, and he claimed that if you just let your everyday thoughts drift in and out of your mind, without paying any real attention to them, your head can become as still as a calm pond, and then you can proceed to get in touch with the good stuff.

When I got back to the flat, after my cosy one-on-one with McFadgen, it was still a couple of hours till Bev was due in from work. I'd knocked about in the town for a while, to give the detective plenty of time to shoot over here and find out that Jinky's flat downstairs was empty, then I'd toddled home, determined to put what I'd heard in the aforementioned documentary into practice.

I'll tell you what, though, it's a hell of a lot harder to empty your mind than the boy up the mountain made it sound.

I sat at the kitchen table with a notebook in front of me, and a pen in my hand, just waiting for all the shite that was zipping about my napper to start settling down and give me a break.

The way I saw it, there were two possible ways I could deal with McFadgen when he finally made contact with Jinky and worked out he'd been off on a wild goose chase. The first would be to give him the name of another thief, somebody else with a strong alibi, who would be just as difficult to track down as Jinky. And the second possibility was to come up with somebody else who might have had another good reason to chib Dougie Dowds, a reason unrelated to his intention to tell McFadgen who had whipped the painting.

So I sat there letting the thoughts about business premises and pink bridesmaids' dresses and beer and inflatable life jackets and fried eggs on pizzas and eastern mystics up mountains float in and out of my mind, waiting for some of the calm pond stuff, and some inspiration about who would be a good candidate to divert McFadgen next.

It was fucking hellish.

The worst of it was, once all the surface bollocks started to fade away, I kept getting plagued with thoughts about Wilma Caldwell, and how my scheme would lead to her marrying a murderer. I didn't seem able to get off that, and I wondered what the boy up the mountain would have recommended under the circumstances. And then I pictured him advising me to shelve the fingerprint idea until I could find a less morally grey way to fund it.

You see what I mean?

Murder polis.

So when there was a knock at the door, loud enough to send a tsunami crashing through the gentle lily pond of my mind, I can't exactly say I was sorry. It even occurred to me that whoever was at the door might be able to banish my thoughts of Wilma Caldwell for a while, and then I'd come back to the notebook with an idea fully formed and ready to go, cooked up by the back bit of the brain while I'd been otherwise distracted.

That was the hopeful state I found myself in as I pushed down on the door handle and twisted the Yale. But, unfortunately, the optimism was short-lived – cause when I opened the door I could tell this particular visitor was unlikely to help clear all thoughts of Wilma Caldwell from my bonce. Owing very much to the fact that it was Wilma Caldwell herself, live and in person, who had decided at this particular moment in time to pay me a visit.

Initially, I was convinced that Wilma had somehow got wind that I was plotting against her future happiness, and she'd come round to have it out with me. No doubt the mountain mystics suffer similar paranoid delusions when they've been abusing their brains the way I'd been abusing mine.

As it turned out, though, she'd only come round to see the wife.

'Is she in?' she asked me as I stood there speechless, probably looking half demented in my confusion.

'Eh . . .' I said, then I got a grip of myself. 'Oh. No. It's usually about six by the time she gets back, Wilma. She'll still be working at the minute.'

'Och,' she said, and she looked at her watch. 'I wanted to thank her for setting me straight the other night. I've brought her these flowers.'

Weirdly, I'd failed to notice she was holding a massive bunch of flowers up until that point. Christ knows how – it was a beast of a thing. It looked like half a bush, with a couple of cabbages stuck in there for good measure. She checked the watch again.

'I'll just come in and wait for her,' she said. 'I might as well. I've got another hour before I have to be at my class.'

And she pushed past me, bold as brass, and stoated off

through the hall towards the kitchen. Before I'd even got the door shut she'd started clattering about in there.

'Where do you keep your vases?' she shouted. 'I'll just get these into some water. I don't want them wilting.'

By the time I'd reached the kitchen myself, there were cupboard doors open and dishes strewn about the work surfaces, and she was down on her knees with the head stuck in a cabinet.

'Are you wanting a cup of tea?' I asked her, and she slowly re-emerged, clutching a vase I'd never seen before, stood up, and reassembled herself.

'That'd be nice,' she said. 'I'll wait for Bev in the living room. Don't let me interrupt whatever you were up to. I'll sit and watch the telly or something.'

She elbowed me out the way of the sink – where I'd been trying to fill the kettle – in order to do her business with the vase, then she took it across to the table and started tearing the wrapping paper off her bizarre floral arrangement.

'What's this you've been working on anyway?' she said, eyeballing my notebook over her shoulder as she did battle with the cellophane. I quickly abandoned the kettle mid-task and hared it across the room to close the book quick smart.

'Just another day at the office,' I told her. 'Pie-in-the-sky stuff. Just a bit of brainstorming.'

'Always in at something, eh, Peacock?' she said as I dumped the book in a drawer. 'Just you get that tea on the go, and then I'll be out your hair. Let you get back to changing the world.'

But as I set up the cups and fished out some teabags, I realised that plan wasn't really going to work. It had been hard enough to get her out of my mind when I'd thought she was on the other side of the city. I was hardly going to be able to plan her downfall while she was sitting on the other side of the wall, watching *Come Dine with Me* in the living room.

'These are looking lovely,' she said. 'What do you think? Do you think Bev'll like them?'

I'd a hard job believing anybody would like them. I couldn't even believe she liked them herself. Maybe Bev was right, and she just went about the place trying to inflict visual misery on the populace. It seemed plausible.

'Aye,' I said. 'They look magic. They'll fair add a bit of life to the room.'

And then it occurred to me that if I had a talk with her about the upcoming wedding, she might say something that would put my mind at rest about her marrying the Vince chap. Maybe she'd say that nothing could ever diminish her love for the guy. Or maybe it would even turn out that she found prison marriages romantic. You never know. Folk you've known for years can have the strangest views they've never dared to air in public. It's a hell of a place, the planet Earth.

'Come and we'll see if we can find a good spot for these flowers in the living room,' I said, when I'd brought the teas to completion. 'I've got as far as I'll get with the brain-storming for one day. Let's go and see how they look through there.'

Wilma Caldwell is a toaty wee thing. When she was married to Brian Caldwell, way back when, they made a striking couple, physically. Brian must be six five, give or take, and his obesity long ago crossed the dividing line between clinical and morbid, in absolutely the wrong direction. Folk often feared he might just sit down on her one night, without noticing she'd nabbed his favourite spot on the couch. There's a good chance that the grounds for divorce Wilma presented in court were simply 'personal safety', or 'to avoid a fatal crushing'.

'Have you seen Beverley in her bridesmaid's dress yet?' she asked me as she positioned the vase on the windowsill, and I told her I had.

'What did you think?' she said. 'She looks amazing in it, doesn't she? Like a film star on the red carpet. Those colours really suit her. And the fit's just perfect. What do you think of it?'

'All of that,' I said. 'Aye. It's a dress and a half, Wilma.'

'If Bev's happy, I'm happy,' she said. 'That's all that really matters. And she told me when she came round the other night that you love the dress as well. Not that I put too much store in your taste in clothes, obviously. But it's a weight off my mind to know that Bev's content.'

'What's up with my taste in clothes?' I asked her. 'Are you having me on? What's that crack about?'

But I don't think she even heard me. She appeared to be off in a world of her own, frowning at some memory or other she was reliving.

'I have to be honest,' she said, 'I was in a right state the other night, Peacock. I really was. I'm a bit embarrassed about it now, but you know how these things can start playing on your mind if you give them half a chance. I'd got myself thoroughly worked up. But Bev was brilliant so she was.'

The dig about my taste in clothes was still rankling me, but I decided to let it go. 'Keep the heid, Peacock,' I told myself, 'You're on a mission here, son. Just let it go, like the boy on the mountain top – in one ear and out the other.'

I knew getting some reassurance she'd be fine shackled to the Vince fellow would be of more benefit to me than defending my reputation as Glasgow's best-dressed ideas man, so I made an effort to screw the nut.

'Were you having some doubts about Vince or something?' I asked her. 'Bev was saying something about that.'

'Och,' she said, 'I got myself into a right old mess so I did. I hardly knew if I was coming or going. I always thought I'd be married to Brian forever. And I got to thinking that if *that* had gone wrong, what was to stop this going wrong. Then I started thinking that maybe me getting married again was hurting Brian more than he was letting on, him still being on his own and that.'

'Did you ask him?'

'I did. He said if I had any doubts at all I should take my time. Which only got me into a bigger muddle. "There's no rush, Wilma," he told me. "If Vince is the right guy, he'll wait for you. He'll wait a year. He'll wait a decade. Don't hurry into anything." So I didn't know what to think.'

I have to admit, the idea of Brian telling her to wait a decade if that's what it took pulled me up a bit short. What a fucking numptie. We'd a business to be cracking on with, and here's him totally easy-oasy about it. 'Get it done and dusted, Wilma. Quick as you like.' That's what I'd have been telling her. It fair shook my faith in the guy's commitment to the project, I don't mind telling you that right here and now.

'But everything's all square?' I asked her, in something of a panic. I think my voice was probably about half an octave higher than its usual register. None too steady either, if I'm being honest. 'What was the problem with Vince anyway?'

'Oh, it was nothing,' she said. 'He'd been acting distant recently. A bit snappy. I got to thinking that maybe I didn't know him quite as well as I'd thought I did. I mean, it's not as if we've known each other that long, relatively speaking. And he'd had a period where he was getting secretive about what he'd been up to, about his comings and goings. No doubt cause I'd got into a routine of badgering him all the time. I probably started acting a bit suspicious of him or something. Bev pointed out he was probably just going through a period of the jitters about the wedding, same as me. She's always that clever, Bev, eh? She's got an answer for everything.'

'Aye, she's very rarely lost for words,' I said.

Wilma nodded slowly and had a go at her tea, while I gave some thought to the Vince chap having become secretive about his activities recently. I'll fucking bet he had. None of this was helping me to feel any more reassured about my current course of action.

'But everything's back to normal now?' I said cheerily. 'All previous misunderstandings have been swept aside, and it's full steam ahead for the big day?'

'All sorted,' she said. 'I confronted him with Bev's idea, that he'd been having second thoughts and getting nervous, and he said that was it in a nutshell. I confessed I'd been going through the same thing, and apologised for being so suspicious. Now we're closer than ever.'

'Brilliant,' I said. 'I'll bet even if the guy ended up in jail now you'd stick by him, eh? It seems like that kind of love story, Wilma. The real thing.'

She frowned and thought about it. I held my breath, waiting for the reassurance that would set me on a clear path to my goals. Just a simple nod would be enough to unhook the back bit of my brain from its concerns with morality, and leave it free to work on a longer-term plan to flummox McFadgen.

I watched and waited for a sign – anything – but unfortunately it never came. At that precise minute Wilma's attention was distracted by the sound of Bev's key skiting about in the Yale lock, and then by the chaos of Bev clattering full-steam into the hallway – and the moment was lost.

A good twenty minutes of hard work right down the tubes.

'Get the kettle on, Peacock,' Bev shouted, dropping her bags on the hall floor and throwing her shoes into the bedroom. 'You wouldn't believe the nightmare I've had trying to get home. Unbelievable. In fact, forget the kettle. Get me a gin and tonic, and put a lemon in it. I've just about had it up to here.'

I got to my feet. I had the feeling she was about to start blowing off steam, and you can never tell where she'll start when she's working her way towards the source of her frustrations. It seemed entirely possible she'd start mouthing off about the bridesmaid's dress, or maybe even Wilma herself, if it took her fancy, so I grabbed the opportunity to nip the situation in the bud.

'You've got a visitor, Bev,' I shouted back. 'Somebody's brought you a wee present. Dive in here for a look while I assemble your gin.'

That did the trick. She was suddenly on her best behaviour and I gave her a quick lift of the eyebrows as I passed her on the way to the kitchen, and watched her tiptoeing her way towards the living-room door.

There was plenty of screaming and shouting while I threw her drink together. Plenty of 'Oh my God'-ing over the flowers, coupled with a healthy helping of 'You shouldn't have', and thankfully by the time I got back in there and handed her her glass she was flopped down on the couch beside Wilma – totally exhausted.

'You look like you've had a day and a half,' Wilma said, and Bev groaned.

'Tell me about it,' she said. 'I'm not just tired, Wilma – I'm sha-*terd*. Bring me that footstool, Peacock.'

I'd half an idea I could still get an answer to my question out of Wilma if I got her back on track quickly enough, so I took my chances while the going looked good.

'I was just saying to Wilma before you came in . . .' I said, but that was as far as I got. As soon as I'd dragged the stool underneath the wife's feet she was off, trampling my good work into oblivion.

'Aren't those flowers just beautiful, Peacock?' she said. 'Have you ever seen anything like them? And all set up in the vase for me coming in. You really didn't need to do that, Wilma.'

'They're just a wee minding after you helping me out the other night,' Wilma said. 'I was telling Peacock how much it meant to me before you came in. I've probably been here for ages. I forgot what time you usually get home so I did, but I decided just to wait. Peacock and me have just been nattering away so we have.'

'Aye,' I said. 'I was just asking Wilma if . . .'

'The trains are to blame,' Bev said. 'I'm usually in a bit earlier, amn't I, Peacock? It's usually plain sailing. I get the train about half five from Central, and I'm usually walking over the bridge about ten minutes later. It's dead handy. Then, tonight, they've put a replacement bus service on. I couldn't believe it. We had to walk all the way down to Jamaica Street to get the bus in the first place, and then it's just chock-a-block all the way down Pollokshaws Road. We hardly moved for about fifteen minutes. Is there football on, Peacock? There must be football on. Or maybe it's something at the Hydro. Bloody awful anyway. And that on top of the afternoon I'd already had. It was non-stop. That job'll be the death of me one of these days, it really will. And that Pat MacKenzie . . . Don't even get me started. Oof!'

She paused for a swipe at the gin and tonic, and Wilma moved closer to her and brushed some of the hair off her brow.

'This is you to blame so it is,' Wilma said, staring at me all of a sudden. 'If she wasn't having to support the two of you, she'd have more time for herself.'

'Eh?'

'You heard me, Peacock Johnson. Don't act it. Look at me when I was married to Brian. It was far from ideal, but he never worked me into the ground the way you're doing to Bev. Brian always paid his own way. *And* the rest.'

'Ach,' Bev said, 'it's not all him to blame, Wilma. Peacock's working on his ideas – something'll come good sooner or later.'

'Will it, though?' Wilma said. 'Will it? I don't think I'd be marrying Vincent if all he had going for him were a few ideas. I know I've had my misgivings over the past few days, but at least I know Vincent'll be able to pay his own way. You'd better be careful you don't end up an old woman before your time, Beverley – working your fingers to the bone while that one's sitting here at the kitchen table scribbling away in his notebook. He even admitted to me himself that what he was working on was pie in the sky. It's time you manned up, Peacock. Look at the state of Bev here. I'm shocked to see her looking like this.'

I was a bit taken aback by this sudden outburst, I have to admit. But I was fucked if I was about to let it go – not a chance. I was suddenly all fired up, and I got myself stuck right in there.

'You don't have a clue *what* I'm working on,' I said. 'Scribbling in the notebook's one thing, but I'm already in the process of setting up a new business. This time next year the wife'll be taking early retirement. Can you see yourself being able to say that with the Vince chap at the helm? Not a chance, Wilma.'

'I can see myself a damn sight more secure than Bev'll be in a year's time, I'll tell you that for nothing so I will. Whatever it is you're working on'll go belly up within a fortnight, like every other daft scheme you've tried to get off the ground. Your ideas are hopeless, Peacock. Every last one of them. And I'm sick of sitting by and seeing Beverley ending up in a state like this. Her mother's right. She's been saying the same thing as me for years. It's time to wake up, Peacock. Smell the coffee.'

Smell the coffee? Jesus Christ. I took a few deep breaths and calmed myself down a touch, just in case I launched into saying something I regretted, regarding the fingerprint start-up, or even regarding her husband-to-be.

'Listen, Wilma,' I said, 'I admit I've had a run of bad luck in the past with a few of my ventures – that's a given – but I'm on to something this time. You don't need to worry about Bev. Seriously. It's under control. We'll be laughing about this in six months time, toasting my success. Wait and see.'

'Oh, I *will* wait and see,' she said. 'I absolutely will. And I'll tell you what – I *hope* you fail. I really do. And I'll tell you why, because the sooner you fail the sooner you can start growing up, and treating Beverly the way you should be treating her. Chipping in. I'm actually *willing* you to fail now so I am. For *everybody's* good.'

Charming, eh? It was something else altogether to sit there listening to her bumming up the qualities of Vince Cowie in contrast to my own failings, knowing what I knew about him, and guessing beyond that to everything else he might be caught up in. Still, I managed to keep that on the back burner.

'You're going to be sorely disappointed if that's your attitude,' I told her. 'No doubt about it. You're in for a bit of a shock when I'm rolling in it this time next year.'

'You'll be lucky if you're not in prison this time next year,' she said, 'what with Duncan McFadgen on your trail night and day.'

'Who told you that?' I said.

'Beverley did.'

'I did not,' Bev said.

'Well, you said he was round here the other night,' Wilma said. 'And Vince has been filling me in on the rest. You're in big trouble if Vince is right, Peacock Johnson. Big trouble.'

'Just as well he's wrong then,' I said, 'about everything.'

'He's right in his assessment of your ideas so he is,' she said. 'As am I. And you've never had a good one in your puff.'

'What about my idea for a record?'

'Rotten.'

'That's not what you said at the time.'

'I was being polite.'

'What about my idea for hiding the adverts on the telly?'

'Mince.'

'Oh for *God's* sake, you two!' the wife suddenly shouted. 'Stop your bickering, will you? I'm just in, my head's splitting, and I'm trying to unwind. Peacock, away downstairs and see wee Jinky or something. Give Wilma and me a bit of peace and quiet to have a nice conversation. Come on, beat it.'

'Jinky's away,' I said. 'He's in Malta. With the Tartan Army.'

She fair perked up a bit at that, the wife. She bounced out of the slouch she'd adopted and sat up straight on the couch. Then she turned towards Wilma and laid a hand on her arm, beaming. 'Wait till I tell you about what happened to wee Jinky. Do you know him? Gordon Jenkins? Peacock's pal that lives down the stair?'

Wilma nodded. 'I do, unfortunately. He was in here that night after my divorce came through.'

'That's right,' Bev said. 'I'd forgotten about his carry-on that night. Anyway, he was flying out to Malta a few days ago to watch Scotland playing . . . Is that right, Peacock?'

I nodded.

'You should've seen him, Wilma,' Bev said. 'All done up in the kilt, saltire painted on his face. I saw him on my way out to work that morning. Eight o'clock and he's standing out on the street all done up like that, a wee tartan bunnet and a football top on, waiting for a taxi, freezing to death. His legs were nearly as blue as his face, and he was chittering away – on the verge of hypothermia it seemed to me. Have you ever seen him in a kilt, Peacock?'

'Not that I remember.'

'Well, he's hardly got the legs for it, I can tell you that. But he was that excited. I stopped to have a quick word with him, and it turned out he'd never been away with the Tartan Army before. This was his first time. He was like a wean going on a school trip to the safari park – totally buzzing.'

She shook her head at the memory, then took a good long drink from the gin and tonic. It was unclear if there was a punchline to the story, or if that was it. You can never tell with the wife – she's as liable to drift off onto another subject as she is to finish any story she starts, and half the time you can never work out if there's any relationship between the place she begun and where she's ended up.

'Is that it?' Wilma said, and Bev shook her head while she was still drinking, the ice cubes rattling about in the glass.

'Wait till you hear what happened,' she said, and she leant forward and put her drink down on the coffee table. 'Jinky got to the airport, two hours before the flight. And after he checked in he got so blootered with his pals in the departure lounge the airline refused to let him on the plane. I saw him in the close on my way out to work this morning. "I thought you were away until next week," I says, and he told me the whole story. He's mortified. Said he's been hiding himself away in the hope nobody would find out. He never even got a refund on his ticket.'

The top of my head went fizzy, as if the blood had been diverted elsewhere, and for a minute I thought I might pass out. Who the fuck gets too drunk to be allowed on a plane? What a fucking tadger.

'So you see,' Bev said, her voice sounding as if it was a couple of hundred yards away, 'there's nothing stopping you going to visit him, Peacock. Away downstairs and give Wilma and me peace for a while.'

'Right,' I said, and got unsteadily to my feet. 'Right, aye.'

My McFadgen plan was fucked. I had to find Jinky quick smart and let him know what I'd let him in for – help him to get his story straight. I grabbed my coat and headed for the door, still feeling like I might keel over at any minute.

'I'll see you when your idea's gone to hell in a handbasket,' Wilma shouted after me, but I didn't even bother to think up a reply. I just wobbled my way down the steps, two and three at a time, hoping to Christ I could find the wee man before McFadgen did.

10

Here's a strange thing.

As I ran about the town looking for Jinky – his girlfriend having told me he'd left the flat early in the morning, and that she hadn't seen him since – I kept becoming aware of this feeling nudging at me that something good had happened. Beneath the outright panic, beneath the chaos in my mind as I tried to work out where to look for Jinky next, and beneath the self-recrimination over the position I'd put the wee man in, there was this other thing going on. This nudging.

I was well aware it wasn't connected to the immediate business at hand – that it had nothing to do with Jinky, or McFadgen – so I did my best to ignore it. I gave my full attention to trying to track the Jinkster down, and ran myself ragged on the city streets, trying to put things right. But all the same, there it was, like a constant companion – this feeling that I'd somehow won a watch or something.

It's a stick-on that when Jinky's not sitting on his arse in his flat, the first place you can usually find him is in the bookies on West Nile Street. It's the bane of my life that whenever he wants to put a bet on we have to traipse halfway across the city just to get to that particular place. It's not even as if there's any special ambience in there, or a crowd of pals that give you a good welcome. It's as characterless as any other chainstore bookies, full of sour faces and antisocial punters. But Jinky's won big there a couple of times, and for that reason he's deemed the place lucky.

'Jinky,' I'm forever telling him, 'you've lost a fucking fortune in there, son. It's just as likely there's a curse on the place.'

But his few big wins have wiped out all semblance of rational judgement on his part, and in the end you have to respect a gambler's superstitions.

'Has he been in yet?' I asked Pete, the permanent fixture behind the counter who looks as if he hasn't seen daylight since about 1975.

'He was in this morning,' he said. 'Haven't seen him since.'

'Did he win?'

Pete shook his head, which was at least a pointer to where he might have gone next. If he'd won, it would be a cert he'd either be in John Jack's casino, trying to ride his luck as far as it would go, or in the arcades at the far end of Sauchiehall Street, doing the same thing. Without the boost of a win he was much more likely to be in one of his usual haunts, and I paid each of them a visit in turn: the Horseshoe Bar, the Vale bar, the shops that were just closing in the Argyll Arcade.

Nothing doing.

It occurred to me that things would have been a hell of a lot easier if the two of us were less paranoid about the tracking possibilities of the mobile phone. I could probably have hunted him down in about five minutes. As it was, by the time I gave the McDonald's on Argyll Street a look, and found it lacking his presence, I realised I was absolutely starving, and I grabbed some chips and a cup of tea for myself, and sat down to revitalise my energy levels.

The place was next to empty – nice and quiet – and as I sat there wondering where in hell the wee man might be, dipping my chips in a wee paper cup of barbecue sauce, the thing that had been nudging at me constantly throughout my travels suddenly made itself fully present. It burst into my consciousness front and centre, in full-blown Technicolor, and I finally understood why it had been making me feel so good, despite everything.

It was nothing other than a realisation, and it was as simple as this: I was off the hook regarding any sense of obligation I'd previously felt towards Wilma Caldwell. If there's one thing I don't take kindly to, it's somebody bad-mouthing my ideas, and Wilma had certainly excelled herself in that department. She'd gone above and beyond the call of duty, in my view. But as it turned out, she'd actually done me a massive favour, cause her slanderous outburst had removed the feelings of guilt I'd been experiencing about letting her walk blindly into her union with Vincent Cowie. Absolutely. Fuck her – that was my attitude to the whole thing now. She was on her own. And on top of that, she'd set me the ultimate challenge: to prove to her that my latest idea would be a massive success.

Challenge accepted.

I felt a muscle that had previously been tight and troubled relaxing somewhere down deep in the recesses of my brain. I was good to go. And even the fact that I'd so far failed to lay my hands on the Jinkster was less distressing, now that a wave of the good stuff was washing over me. I'd find Jinky. No question. Before the night was out, I'd have tracked him down, explained the situation to him, and we'd have worked out a way to keep him hidden from McFadgen for a few more days. And I'd fall asleep ticking over the problem of who to send McFadgen off in pursuit of next, drifting into oblivion like a baby.

I took a right good swallow of my sugary tea, put paid to the remainder of my chips, and then I sat back in my seat and gave some thought to where I could look for Jinky next. The longer I sat there, though, the more I started to get the weird feeling that there was actually somebody sitting next to me, at my own table, in a seat I'd been sure was empty just a few minutes earlier. I paid some attention to my peripheral vision, and the more I did the more I became certain there was some mad bastard sitting there – hardly moving, hardly breathing. And in the end the tension got too much for me, and I swung right round to examine exactly what was going on. And I'd been right. Dead on. There *was* somebody sitting beside me, staring into space, happy as Larry. And that somebody – are you ready for this? – that somebody, was Detective Inspector Duncan McFadgen.

As I live and breathe.

'Have you been looking for Gordon Jenkins?' McFadgen asked me. Straight in. No preliminaries, no 'fancy bumping into you here', not even a casual hello. Just immediately down to business.

It took me a minute to work out whether I was coming or going, but then I was on it. 'I told you earlier,' I said. 'We're far from being on speaking terms these days.'

'I'm well aware of what you told me earlier,' McFadgen said, 'but it hardly matches up with your recent actions. You've spent the past hour and a half nipping in and out of Jinky's favourite haunts. Am I wrong?'

I turned round and glared at the guy. I was seriously starting to wonder if he'd had me microchipped, so he could follow my movements via GPS. It was unbelievable.

'You're way off,' I told him. 'If I don't see Jinky till the middle of the next century it'll still be too soon. I've had it with the clown. Totally.'

McFadgen got up out of his seat and moved round to the other side of the table to sit facing me. The lights in McDonald's are never particularly flattering, but they definitely had it in for McFadgen. I was glad I'd already finished my chips. He'd have put me right off them otherwise.

'If that's the truth,' he said, 'then this is your lucky day. Cause I can pretty much guarantee you won't be seeing him for a good few years. We've got him down at the station right now, and I'd be willing to stake my reputation on the fact that he won't be coming out again.'

I adopted the poker face. Jinky would be in a right stinker with me for weeks about this, no question. I'd have to go to a hell of a length to make it up to him, but at least McFadgen would look like a right plum when the matter of Magaluf finally raised its napper.

'You got him on the painting?' I said. 'You've got to hand it to John Jack, eh? He rarely puts a foot wrong.'

McFadgen smiled. Not a good move considering the harshness of the fluorescent lighting. Not a good look for him in there at all. I don't think I'd ever noticed how truly gruesome his teeth were before. Far from pretty – let's just leave it at that.

'You know we didn't get him on the painting,' he said. 'And you know we won't. Do you think I zip up the back, Johnson? Honestly? My guess is you only just found out Gordon failed to make it to Malta. And I'm pretty sure that's how come you've been haring about the town trying to track him down, hoping you can warn him what's going on before I get to him. But I got to him. Hours ago. He was in the Vale bar. A good two-and-a-half hours before you even thought about looking in there. And it didn't take long to establish that he was in Magaluf at the time that painting was stolen. What kind of operation do you think I'm running here? Some kind of training course for mentally challenged cadets?'

I had to admit, from where I was sitting, that was exactly how it looked.

'So you've arrested him for doing something that happened while he was thousands of miles away?' I said. 'How the hell does that work?'

'It works like this,' McFadgen said. 'Nobody's claiming we arrested him for stealing the painting. Like we both know, he's got a stone-cold alibi to prove otherwise. But the thing he hasn't got, importantly, is an alibi for the twenty-third of June between the hours of seven and ten o'clock. And that's why, barring the formalities, he's been arrested for the murder of Dougie Dowds. And I reluctantly have to admit I've got you to thank for helping us make that arrest.'

This news hit me like a full-on kick in the stones. The pain was actually physical. And it was a mindbender on top of that – a real brain-melter – I couldn't make head nor tail of it.

'Wait a wee minute here, McFadgen,' I said. 'I don't think I'm quite following you, pal. You're telling me John Jack was havering when he said Jinky took that painting, right? Fair play, I can just about buy that. Everybody's capable of making a mistake once in their life. But how are you getting from the fact that Jinky was in Magaluf when the painting was stolen to the idea that he murdered Dougie Dowds? I think I must have missed a step or two.'

McFadgen employed that manky smile again. 'I told you,' he said. 'He's unable to confirm his whereabouts on the evening in question. He's got no alibi.'

I stared at him while the wheels of my brain spun chaotically.

'Listen, McFadgen,' I said, 'I told you I'd be happy enough to see Jinky locked up for nicking that picture. That's a given. The guy's nothing but a thorn in my side at the minute. But standing by while he gets a life sentence is something else again. You're just after telling me that the reason you've been suspecting me's because I *have* got an alibi. You've been telling me that's an anomaly – that folk can very rarely prove where they were at any given time – so what the hell's going on here? If the only thing you've got on Jinky's the fact that he's devoid of an alibi, how the hell can that mean anything? By your own reckoning?'

'It can't,' McFadgen said. 'And it wouldn't, if that was all I had on him. But it's not all I've got, is it?'

'It looks hell of a like it to me.'

152

He shook his head. 'What I've got, Johnson, is this. I've got one guy with a cast-iron alibi for the time a highly valuable painting was stolen. I've got a murder victim who was on the verge of telling me who had stolen that painting, just before he was killed. And then I've got another guy with a cast-iron alibi for the time this informant was murdered. Now, when you take into account that these two guys with the unbreakable alibis are a long-term double act, and that one of them has just spent the past couple of hours charging about Glasgow with the intention of informing the other that I'm about to start questioning him, that seems like a hell of a coincidence, does it not? Surely I'd have to be some kind of deranged lunatic to refrain from drawing the obvious conclusions from that pile of evidence. No?'

McFadgen's unique brand of faulty logic had rarely failed to astound me in the past, but this was something else altogether. This was a guy on the precipice of a full-scale mental collapse, it seemed to me.

'I'm inclined to adhere to the opposite point of view, McFadgen,' I said. '*Coming* to that conclusion seems to me the work of a deranged lunatic. Are you for real? Seriously?'

He wiggled about in his seat and leant across the table towards me. 'I told you I'd get you,' he said. 'And the way I see it now, you've got two options. You can either admit that you killed Dougie Dowds and save your daft pal from rotting away in Barlinnie for the rest of his life, or you can leave me to question Gordon for a few days – let me convince him he'll get a sizeable chunk of time off for helping us to bring in whoever stole that painting, and I'll get you that way. Your choice. Are you in the mood for doing the right thing?'

I knew it was going to be far from pleasant, getting even closer to McFadgen's bulbous face and bogging teeth under the harsh fluorescent lights, but I bit the bullet and aped the way he was leaning forward, to meet him in the middle of the table.

'You're full of shit, McFadgen,' I said. 'And on top of that, you've got nothing. You're like a hard-wired conspiracy theorist, connecting the dots where no connection exists, identifying patterns where there *are* no patterns. You're on to plums, pal. Nothing doing.'

He leant back, thankfully, cause he'd started in on the mad grinning again. Then he slowly rearranged his jacket and got to his feet.

'You know where to find me when you change your mind,' he said. 'Unless I've already come for you first, with a signed confession from your pal.'

He wandered up to the counter and stood waiting while they served him a cup of coffee. There was a big ketchup stain on the tail of his jacket, and I looked at the rest of it smeared about on the seat he'd just vacated.

What a fucking tumshie.

He was attempting some light-hearted banter with the

girl at the counter, but he was the only one laughing. She was just looking severely embarrassed, trying her best to smile back at him as she handed him his change.

'I'll be seeing you sooner than you think, Johnson,' he said as he breezed past the table again. 'In highly pleasurable circumstances, for me at least.'

Then the chump was gone, and I sat on and digested the shitty news he'd left behind him.

There was very little left of the warm glow I'd been feeling immediately before he appeared, I can tell you that. The fact that I'd managed to unburden myself of my Wilma Caldwell guilt really wasn't doing that much for me anymore. It had been totally superseded by the fact that I'd landed my best pal in the jail. For murder, no less.

I started to wonder for the first time if this fingerprint-erasing enterprise would really turn out to be worth all the havoc it had caused me – if it would justify me having laid waste to the lives of so many innocent bystanders. And then something else began to vie for my attention, another consideration. I could tell it wasn't going to be a jolly thought, and for a few minutes I did what I could to pretend it wasn't there. I tried to get my attention onto the subject of how I could get wee Jinky out of McFadgen's clutches, but this thing was relentless. It just kept badgering me, coming at me from all angles, until finally there it was, fully formed, sitting right behind my eyes in all its glory. And its proposition was this: what if Jinky actually knew who had stolen that painting from Pollok House? What if he knew it was Vince Cowie?

You see the enormity of that?

If McFadgen started offering him preferential treatment in return for that information, and if Jinky had already come into possession of the facts, via John Jack for example, then that would be everything fucked.

The more I sat there and thought about it, the more it seemed highly likely to me that McFadgen didn't even really believe his bampot double-alibi conspiracy theory. I mean, who would? It started to seem more plausible that he'd just taken Jinky in to try and frighten him into revealing that I'd stolen that painting, in exchange for letting him go. He'd no doubt spin Jinky the tale that I'd done everything in my power to frame him, up to and including grassing him up to McFadgen for the theft of the picture. And maybe McFadgen even thought if all else failed I'd step up and do the decent thing to get the wee man off the hook – turn myself in.

The exact ins and outs were, in a way, purely academic. The pertinent point was that McFadgen would squeeze Jinky for that painting data, and if Jinky had it to give he would eventually spill it. And I couldn't let that happen. I couldn't let McFadgen get his hands on Vince Cowie before the wedding, not after all the shite I'd put up with to get to this stage.

I got up and dumped my cup and my chip poke into one of the bins, and then I got myself out onto the streets.

Motion was what was needed – I needed to be moving to get the juices flowing, to get the blood rattling round my brain. The best ideas always come to me when I'm in motion, and the idea I was in need of now was going to have to be one of the best I'd ever had. How in the name of Christ do you stop a fragment of information passing between two bodies who are locked away together behind closed doors – in the interrogation room of a secure police unit – one of them no doubt skilled in the art of extracting vital intelligence, and the other one ready and willing to give it just so he can get home to his bed?

Something of a brain-tickler, I think you'll agree.

I strode along Argyll Street at a fair old pace, just about breaking into a jog as I turned up onto Queen Street, then slowing down slightly on Buchanan Street cause the hastily consumed chips were beginning to bring on a stitch. God alone knows how long I walked for. All that mattered to me was getting the adrenaline buzzing, getting the synapses firing, getting the back bit of the brain working away on all cylinders. It was a hell of a task that lay ahead of me – I was under no illusions about that – but I'm an ideas man, it's what I do, it's what I've always done. And I knew that if I stuck with it long enough, and just kept walking and walking, I was giving myself every chance that I possibly could. And that's the best you can do under any circumstances, eh?

Just keep the brain ways open, and keep the faith.

11

The idea, when it finally came, was a monster. An absolute behemoth. I mean, I've had some belters in my time, but this one impressed even me.

The only question was whether it had arrived too late. It had fair taken its time in turning up, I can tell you that.

I'd got nothing during all the time I'd spent charging about the city centre, and in the end I'd decided to walk home – across the Jamaica Bridge and all the way down Pollokshaws Road. That's no idle stroll, I can assure you. But as I clambered my way up the stairs to the flat, on the verge of collapse, I was still entirely empty-handed. I sat staring at the telly for a couple of hours, listening to the wife nattering away, hoping that the surface distractions would allow my unconscious to do the business. But by the time I flopped into bed I was still right where I'd been when I left McDonald's: fucking nowhere.

It was a hell of a night – the tossing and the turning, the

staring at the patch of light on the ceiling that had sneaked in through a crack in the curtains. Brutal. But after the wife had gone to work, and I'd continued to lie there slipping in and out of fuzzy dreams, it finally occurred – the revelation.

Here's the thing, though – it didn't come to me the way these things have come in the past. It didn't form itself slowly in the darker parts of the psyche, finally announcing itself in a blaze of glory, fully assembled. Far from it. All that happened was this – I was lying there defeated, convinced Jinky must have cracked by now, and I started going over the shite McFadgen had been spouting, when I clocked that McFadgen himself had told me exactly what to do, in plain speech. Not hinted at it, or said something that fired off a series of associations in my mind that led to the ultimate solution, just actually said it: 'You can either admit that you killed Dougie Dowds and save your daft pal from rotting away in Barlinnie for the rest of his life, or . . .'

Et cetera, et cetera.

Simple as that. The very nugget I'd been looking for, and I sprang out of bed at a clip, hoping against hope that I might still have time to put the thing into action.

Here's how I saw it . . .

As long as Jinky hadn't spilled the beans yet regarding Vince Cowie's involvement, I could simply approach McFadgen, tell him he'd been right all along, and claim that the guilt of landing the Jinkster in the shit had finally been too much for me, and that I was here to confess. No doubt I'd have to put up with a sickening level of self-congratulation on McFadgen's part, but that was the only real downside. All other investigation into the matter would cease for the time being, Vince Cowie would be in the clear, the wedding would progress unimpeded, and once it was all done and dusted, fully binding in the eyes of God and the eyes of the law, I could get John Jack to unleash the truth about Vince and get me out of there.

The funny thing was, I realised this idea was so solid I could have put it into practice a hell of a lot earlier and saved myself a bucketload of grief. If I'd just cottoned on to it as soon as John Jack told me who stole the picture, I could have been quietly tucked away in a nice cell somewhere ever since, instead of spending my time lurching from nervous breakdown to nervous breakdown, as had been the case.

That's the measure of the best ideas, though – they're always blindingly obvious in retrospect. You can never work out how come some bastard never thought of them sooner.

Look at the paperclip.

Case in point.

I threw on my clothes and dived outside to find a taxi. At a rough estimate it was about nineteen hours since they'd hauled Jinky in. He'd already been deprived of one night's sleep, which might hardly matter in the case of most folk, but this was the Jinkster we were talking about, not the toughest of customers at the best of times. And to further add to the tension, I'd still a quick trip to make to John Jack's place, to fill him in on the plan that would prevent me rotting away in a jail cell for the rest of my days, utterly abandoned.

'Can you pick it up a bit, pal?' I said to the taxi driver as he dawdled along the riverside as if we were on a sightseeing tour. But all that served to do was encourage him to take things at an even more leisurely pace than beforehand.

The sweat was soaking through my shirt by the time I burst into John Jack's office, waving at him to get off the phone. He gave me the finger and carried on wittering for what seemed like another half hour, but was probably only a couple of minutes, and the second he hung up I unleashed my pitch, forgoing any run-up or semblance of social niceties.

I talked without hardly taking a breath, the words gushing out at such a rate that even *I* began to wonder if they were making any sense. I laid the whole plan out for him, telling him that as soon as Wilma and Vince left for their honeymoon he was to call McFadgen in and alert him to the reality of the situation, and that he was to phone Bev at her work in a couple of hours from now and let her know what had happened to me, and assure her it was all a daft mistake, and that he was already working on finding out who the real villain was, and that he'd have me out of the jail in no time. When I finished J.J. just pulled a cigar out of his drawer, lit it up, sat back in his chair shaking his head, and said, quite matter-of-factly, 'I don't think I like it, Peacock.'

I'll be perfectly honest with you, I just about lost the nut at that point. No word of a lie.

'What the fuck are you talking about?' I shouted at him. 'What do you mean you don't like it? Get a grip, John. It's a peach, pal. It's one of the best ideas I've ever had.'

But the big man just sat there quietly, watching me. He puffed at the cigar and tapped it on the edge of his ashtray. Then he repeated himself. 'I don't like it,' he said. 'Simple as that. It's too risky.'

'How is it risky?' I said. 'The only risk involved is me standing here talking to you when I should be out there stopping Jinky fucking everything up. That's the only way it can possibly fail. I appreciate your concern for my wellbeing, John, but it's hardly your place to decide what risks I take or don't take. I'm a big boy, pal.'

He frowned at me. 'You're attributing a level of concern to me that I don't deserve,' he said. 'I don't give a flying fuck whether there's any risk to you involved or otherwise. Far from it. You can get yourself into whatever mess you want. The bigger the better, as far as I'm concerned. What I'm talking about here is the risk involved for *me*. I don't want any dealings with McFadgen. At all. If I make the slightest contact with him he's bound to start sniffing around me for all kinds of other reasons, and that's something I don't need. That's the risk I'm talking about. And that's the risk I'm not willing to take.'

I felt about ready to explode. I clenched my fists, feeling like I might be on the verge of a massive coronary, and then, suddenly, a huge wave of calm washed over me. I'd connected again. It must have been something to do with the fact that I was wound up to high doh, the adrenaline greasing the wheels and what not, but I'd just had another blinder.

'Rab Clark,' I said, not even bothering to formulate my thoughts before I started speaking. 'You've been itching to get info from him since the minute he was banged up. Am I right? If I spend a couple of weeks in there with him, I'll be in the perfect position to pump him for it. And once you get me back out again, I'll be able to bring it straight to your door.'

He knew I'd got him. He tried to hide it for a minute, but there was no way he was about to pass up on an opportunity like this.

'You're a bastard,' he said in the end. Short and sweet. He was totally fuming.

'Phone the wife after six,' I said. 'And contact McFadgen as soon as Wilma and Vince are airborne. I don't want to spend a minute longer under lock and key than I need to.'

I started heading for the door while the big man took a

good deal of his frustration out on his cigar, chewing at it in a way that suggested it was a surrogate for my intestines. It was clear he was itching to score some kind of point against me to make himself feel better, but I didn't have time to stand about waiting for his lumbering brain to kick into gear.

I pulled the door open.

'What about Brian Caldwell?' he said.

'What about him?'

'If you think I'm filling him in on your pish plan you're up a gum tree,' he said. 'McFadgen and Bev are my limit. I swore years ago I'd never talk to Caldwell again. I'm hardly about to break that vow for you.'

I shrugged. 'Fair enough,' I said. 'He'll find out the truth soon enough, when I get back out again.'

'Unless he's already decided to invest his cash in something else by then, having assumed you're serving a life sentence and what not. Something to think about on your quiet nights after lock-up anyway, I'd imagine.'

He gave me a fuck-you grin with the cigar still clamped between his teeth and I battered my way down the stairs and out onto the street, immediately on the lookout for a taxi. What a prick, man. All of a sudden he had me in a right fucking tizz. I checked my watch. If he hadn't made me go all round the houses getting his agreement to do me two simple favours I'd probably still have had the time to make a quick detour to Brian's place, to fill him in on the situation. As it was, I couldn't take a chance on it stopping me getting to McFadgen before Jinky cracked. The trouble was, though, the big fat snidey bastard was right. There was every possibility that on hearing the news about my incarceration, Brian would make alternative plans for his alimony windfall. Not least of all since he might find the idea of going into business with a cold-blooded killer somewhat unpalatable.

A taxi with its light on breezed towards me on the other side of the road, and I stuck my arm up in the air. The driver tried to pretend he never saw me, so I charged out into the traffic and called his bluff.

'Here you!' I shouted. 'Get a grip.'

He did the staring-straight-ahead thing, but then the lights changed and he was suddenly at a standstill, stuck there like a total doolie. I pulled his back door open and jumped in.

'Take me to the police station on Stewart Street,' I said. 'Quick as you like.'

The most probable scenario with Brian Caldwell was that he'd think our business was fucked when he heard about my arrest, but that his finances would still be available by the time I got out again. Surely. It was just John Jack trying to get in about me, to stop himself feeling bad about the fact that I'd played him like a violin. I mean, who finds another goldmine to invest in within the space of a fortnight? Everything was sure to turn out for the good.

'Do you want me go the Expressway, or via Charing Cross?' the charioteer asked.

'Which way's quicker?'

'Hard to tell at this time. Six and two threes.'

I thought about it, and I thought about lying on my jail bunk every night, torturing myself with the thought of Brian Caldwell's financial infidelity, and all the other mad stuff he might have found to commit his money to in my absence. And I looked at my watch again.

'Fuck it,' I said. 'Turn it around. Take me out to Maryhill. There's been a change of plan.'

He voiced his displeasure in a wordless grunt and started causing havoc amongst his fellow road users by spinning the cab around in the middle of the street.

'And pick it up a bit,' I told him. 'Less of the bewildered-pensioner-on-a-Sunday-afternoon act, and a bit more of the boy racer. I'm on a schedule here, pal. Let's get a jildy on.'

12

Concision – that would have to be the watchword here. Just get in, get to the point, and then get straight back out again. The thing was, it had struck me I'd need to present Brian with an alternative explanation for why I was doing what I was about to do. Charging in there and telling him I was about to turn myself in to make sure his ex-wife ended up married to a murderer might not be the most advantageous way to go about things. A more subtle approach would probably be required. Just to be on the safe side.

'Are you wanting me to wait?' the taxi driver asked when we finally pulled up at the kerb outside Brian's place. 'Are you wanting me to take you on to Stewart Street when you're done here?'

'I'd be quicker dragging myself there on my belly,' I told him, and pushed a tenner through the wee hole in the Perspex. 'Keep the change, pal. That's you discharged.'

The journey had been a bloody nightmare. I'd half started to wonder if he even had a licence at one point. It seemed like he must have sat his test on a milk float, the speed he drove at. We barely broke the ten-mile-an-hour mark the whole way there.

'There's no change to keep,' he said as I opened the door. 'The fare's twelve quid.'

I fished out another fiver and then ejected myself. If Jinky'd already cracked by the time I reached the police station, I'd know who to blame.

This guy.

Even out on the kerb I thought he'd decided just to keep sitting there, till I noticed he was actually moving, almost imperceptibly. Shuddering off into the flow of traffic, while I stood getting my story straight for Brian.

It didn't take me long. Rab Clark, that was the solution. John Jack was sending me into the belly of the beast for a couple of weeks, to get him some information from Rab Clark.

'So don't worry about our joint endeavour if you hear I've been lifted, Brian,' I'd say. 'It's purely temporary, strictly a set-up. As soon as I've got the lowdown from Rab, John Jack'll point the law in the direction of the real villain and I'll be out of there again.'

And the best of it was, if he asked, I could feign ignorance about who was guilty of the crime I was owning up to – say J.J. wouldn't tell me in case I freaked out in prison and spilled the beans to get myself released, before I'd completed the job at hand.

Lovely.

Then when Vince actually went down, my record would remain unblemished in Brian's eyes. The responsibility for ruining Wilma's future would fall entirely at John Jack's feet. Fair and square.

I was already halfway up the path by the time I'd it fully figured out. No hanging about when he answered the door, that was the main thing. I pushed the bell and stood there waiting, rehearsing my bit, editing it down – 'I'm in a right rush, Brian. This is just a quick heads up. Neither business nor pleasure, just a wee warning.'

He's got one hell of a pad, the Brian Caldwell chap. It makes you feel good just to be associated with the guy. Big detached job, huge garden, gravel driveway. What it always says to me is this is where you're heading, Peacock, now that you're going into business with this guy. Out of the manky Southside flat and into a place like this. No problem. From what I understand, the reason he got to keep it when Wilma and him split up was because he runs his architect's business from there. Lives there and works there. So he paid a premium in alimony to be allowed to keep it.

You can see how you'd end up attached to a place like that. Absolutely. If Jinky broke down under McFadgen's questioning and stood between me and a place like this, he'd better fucking watch himself – that's all I could think. Hang in there, Jinky, son – just another half hour. Forty-five minutes at the outside. Breathe deeply, Jinks – withhold the information.

Your pal Peacock's on his way.

I watched the light coming on in the hallway and Brian's misty shape moving towards me behind the frosted glass. He was wearing something yellow – a jumper or a cardigan.

'Hurry up,' I muttered to myself, and then he was there – door open, big smiles. We were good to go.

If there's one thing you can say about Brian Caldwell, it's this – the bastard can fair talk. He'd already started talking before he even opened the door, and before I could interrupt him he'd turned and was halfway back down the hall, muttering something about cavolo nero.

'It's just coming to the boil,' he informed me. 'Just in here. The advice was to chiffonade the leaves prior to blanching. That's what the recipe says anyway.'

'I was just . . .' I shouted, but he'd turned towards an open doorway and disappeared. I'd been intending to give him the full pitch right there on the doorstep. The last thing I'd wanted to do was cross the threshold, but I couldn't see any avoiding it. I could still hear him yabbering away – seemingly under the impression that I'd followed him in – so I was forced to do just that. I whacked the door shut behind me and jogged towards the room he'd gone into, determined to disrupt his monologue.

'I'm just following a video some guy posted online,' he said. 'Who knows how it'll turn out. By rights, I should really be working. I've got a commission with a deadline for a week on Wednesday, but it's been driving me daft. You need a break sometimes. So I thought I'd give the cavolo nero a go. See how it turns out. That's the worst thing about living and working in the same place, too many distractions. And then again, you never really clock off. You're always working. Hang on . . . let me just turn the heat up a bit.'

'Brian,' I said, 'I'm only here for a minute. I'm on a schedule. I've . . .'

'Ah,' he said, 'the joint venture. How's it coming along? Are we looking good? You were saying you're still scouting potential venues. How are things looking? I was talking to Sandy Boyle the other day, and he was telling me about a new place out near the Barras. Sounded promising. And discreet. Let me think now, how much was it he said they were asking? It seemed pretty reasonable.'

Now, to be honest, I should probably have taken a few deep breaths at this point and then had another go at drawing the guy's attention to the immediacy of the situation, in a reasonable and controlled manner. But I was just about at the end of my rope. John Jack's dithering, the taxi driver apparently strung out on Temazepam, and now this – it had me rammed up to the limit. At that very moment, Jinky could be deciding that all that mattered in the world was sleep, and he could be making up his mind to give them whatever they wanted, just for a chance to lie down and drift off into the dreamless. So I suppose I saw red. And I suppose, with the benefit of hindsight, I maybe went a wee bit overboard.

'For fuck's sake, Brian, shut the fuck *up*!' I roared. Full voice, mind. And so close to him that I could see wisps of his hair blowing back in the blast. 'This is *serious*, pal. I'm not here on a social visit. I'm not here to learn about the finer points of boiling a fucking *cabbage*. This is life or death, Brian. Pay a*ttention*, son.'

I don't suppose you can really blame the guy for the look that appeared on his face. He was fair taken aback, I can tell you that. But give him his due, he didn't accept matters lying down. The boy stood his ground. He straightened himself up to his full height and took a step closer towards me. He did at least shut the fuck up for a minute, though, there was that to be said for my efforts – I'd at least managed to achieve my aim.

I took quick advantage of the situation, and dived in there before he got started up again.

'Wee Jinky,' I said. 'Right? He's been nabbed. He's currently sitting in a police cell, courtesy of a detective inspector by the name of McFadgen. He's . . .'

I realised I'd lost my train of thought. I was going into jail at the request of John Jack – that was the message I was here to deliver. But I'd got myself into a hell of a mess, no doubt owing to the highly charged atmosphere and the urgent need for me to be on my way.

'McFadgen's convinced Jinky killed a boy called Dougie Dowds,' I said. 'But I know otherwise. That's what I'm here to tell you. That's what we need to be talking about, Brian. Not whatever's going on with your pot there. Not whether I've found us premises yet. Are you understanding me? This is serious business, Brian. Jinky's sitting in there, right now, fighting for his life, and meanwhile you're . . .'

A horrific burst of pain exploded on the inside of my skull, and all of a sudden I was helpless. One minute, I appeared to be standing up staring Brian in the face, the next I'd come to with a different view of the room altogether, convinced beyond all doubt that I must have had a stroke, or something of that nature. Brian was standing over me, peering at me in a puzzled manner, and I didn't seem to be able to move. I was dizzy as fuck, everything sort of spinning, and I tried to lift a hand up to touch my head, to grab at where the pain was centred.

Nothing doing.

The will was there. As far as I could tell I was sending the signal to the desired limb, but that's where the whole operation hit a brick wall. The arm itself refused to obey the command. So I switched my thinking to the other arm and gave that a go instead – same story. No response.

I became certain then that I must have blown something serious in my overheated brain. Thinking about it logically, it was hardly surprising – the ideas had been coming thick and fast ever since I'd had the big one about giving myself up to McFadgen. And on top of that, there'd been the constant stress of trying to get to McFadgen before Jinky snapped, and never quite managing it.

I tried to focus more intently on the Brian chap. Everything was still hell of a fuzzy, but he was continuing to lean in towards me, squinting at me, and I realised there was a further consequence to this unfortunate development. Me having the stroke had left the way clear for him to get a word in edgewise again, and he was taking full advantage of the opportunity. As his image sharpened I clocked that he was talking – non-stop. And although things were sounding as if I'd been submerged in a tank of gloop, I tried to get a handle on what he was saying.

'I don't know what to do,' I heard. And something like, 'What did you have to do that for?' And then again, 'What am I supposed to do, Peacock? Eh? What can I do?'

In the main, I was getting two messages. One, he was in a right panic about how to go about helping me, and two, he definitely seemed to be berating me for having fallen victim to this debilitating malady.

'Why?' he was shouting. 'What did you have to do it for?'

Which hardly seemed all that compassionate under the circumstances. It seemed a bit harsh. I could understand his anxiety at having to deal with me in this state, especially since he seemed at such a loss as to how to go about it. But I felt it was something he could have made more of an effort to keep to himself, rather than crouching over me, bawling into my face like that. It didn't really strike me as the most empathetic bedside manner I'd ever encountered.

'Calm yourself,' I tried to say. And my full expectation was that nothing would materialise at my lips, given the earlier fiasco with the arms. But as it turned out, my voice didn't seem to have been impaired. I still had the power of speech, and I heard myself saying the intended words quite clearly. Not that they'd any effect on the ranter – he was still in full flow. But the whole thing instilled me with a certain level of confidence. The dizziness eased off a notch, the vision sharpened up to full whack, and my hearing began to return to normal.

'What would you do in my position?' the bold one was shouting. 'Eh? Consider that. Ask yourself that question, and see what you come up with. You've put me in a very difficult place, Peacock. My back's against the wall. Why did you have to . . .'

He backed away from me at this point and stood up properly. Then he turned his back to me and started pacing about.

'I think I might be all right, Brian,' I said. 'I think everything might be okay.'

And then I suddenly realised that it absolutely wasn't.

Seriously.

It wasn't even close.

You see, I wasn't lying on the floor, like I'd thought I was. I was sitting in a chair. And it wasn't that my hands had been refusing to obey my commands earlier, it was that my hands were taped behind my back. As tight as fuck. And my ankles were taped to the legs of the chair. There was a dirty wad of tape wrapped around my chest six or seven times, securing me to the chair's back, and then I noticed that the pot that had been boiling away on the cooker when I came in was now lying couped on the floor, the muck that had been in it strewn about the place. And it came to me that this pot was no doubt the source of the horrendous pain in my napper, and that Brian – God bless him – must have skelped me with it, just seconds before I'd passed out.

He picked another pot up from the worktop now, and hurled it at the far wall, shouting four colours of abuse at it as it careered across the floor behind me. Certainly disconcerting, don't get me wrong, but I was somewhat preoccupied with my own wee psychodrama at the time, and his outburst had less effect on me than you might imagine. You see, I was in the middle of rejoicing at the realisation that I hadn't actually had a stroke while at the same time dealing with the reality that there was no possible chance of me ever getting to Jinky in time now – what with the duct tape and the unhinged maniac making it quite clear he'd be keeping me here for the foreseeable future. Swings and roundabouts, I suppose. They say you always get the yin and the yang at times of great upheaval.

Your man Brian seemed to have managed to unburden himself of a good deal of frustration during his latest tantrum, though, and he calmed down somewhat and came to stand in front of me again.

'I'm going to have to kill you,' he said, with a touch of regret in his voice – and although I appreciated that slight concession, his statement still fair took the shine off the elation I'd been feeling about the fact that I hadn't had a stroke.

'How come?' I said, and he came over a bit shirty, like he was a school teacher and I'd drifted off for a while during one of his boring lessons.

'Self-preservation,' he said. 'Obviously. Do you think I'm going to stand by and let a lowlife like you drag me down? Honestly? It's you or me, Peacock, and since I'm the one in the position of power here, I'm afraid it's going to have to be you. What did you have to get involved for anyway? What the hell did Dougie Dowds matter to you? Surely he was as much of a thorn in your side as he was anyone else's?'

'I don't think I'm quite following you, Brian,' I said. 'It might be something to do with the massive blow to the head I've just sustained, but I don't seem to be thinking quite as clearly as usual. What in the name of fuck are you talking about?'

'He was a grass,' Brian said. 'An informer. Don't tell me you never knew that. You must have done. But contrary to what you might think, it wasn't my intention to hurt him. Not at all. I only went round to his flat to try and talk some sense into him, and things got heated. That's the truth. All I wanted to do was convince him to keep quiet about a painting. I offered him money. We argued about the amount. He started getting aggressive, and we got into it. That's all that happened, with God as my witness.'

I have to admit, I was struggling to keep up – which is pretty much always the case when Brian starts spouting – but the unexpected nature of what I was hearing was playing a part in my befuddlement as well, as was my burgeoning concussion, no doubt.

'I know you probably think I'd gone out there with the specific intention of . . . whatever,' he said, 'but you're wrong. It was an accident, pure and simple. We ended up struggling out on the balcony, and then I just got the better of him. I don't think I even realised at that point we'd ended up outside. Then I just overpowered him, and he fell. And I ran.'

He was looking a bit teary now, in actual fact. He wiped his nose on the back of his hand, and I just stared at the guy, stunned, finally grasping what he was talking about. Finally on it.

'Eh . . .' I said, feeling a tad awkward as a couple of tears rolled down his cheeks. 'I think you've maybe jumped the gun a bit here, Brian. I think you've maybe got a bit ahead of yourself. I only came round to tell you I was going to be spending a couple of weeks in the slammer to get wee Jinky out of there. And to do a favour for John Jack. This whole revelation is totally news to me, pal. I'm thinking you've maybe given me credit for something a touch beyond my capabilities.'

'But . . .' he said, and his eyes widened, to an extreme degree in fact. And his face went as white as the face of a corpse. 'But when you shouted at me you said . . .' He stopped and he thought, no doubt rerunning the earlier conversation in his mind and trying to see it from a different angle.

'I think it's been a case of crossed wires,' I said. 'Mixed messages. It's easily done, I suppose.'

Embarrassing, I have to admit. To be frank, I hardly knew where to look. He'd make a cock-up of epic proportions, and he knew it.

He put his head in his hands and just stood there, totally silent. It struck me that if there'd been somebody mooching about in the garden at that minute, and they'd happened to look in through the window, they'd have seen one hell of a strange sight – me sitting there trussed up with the duct tape, firmly attached to the kitchen chair, him standing in front of me with his face covered, slowly rocking backwards and forwards. It would have taken quite a bit of surmising to work out what the fuck was going on, I was certain of that. Still, eventually he got a grip on himself, and he re-emerged from behind his mitts in a more collected state of being.

'So you never knew I killed Dougie when you came here?' he asked. 'When you said, "I'm here to put things right", you didn't even have an inkling?'

I shook my head. 'Not a clue,' I said, and, strangely, he looked like a great weight had been lifted from him. It was as if we'd gone back to that point in time, and he seemed to think that was still how things stood. He apologised for having skelped me on the skull with the ironmongery, and he seemed like his old self for a second or two, then reality apparently caught up with him, and his face darkened again.

'But you know now . . .' he said, and I admitted there was no getting away from that singularly uncomfortable fact.

'I certainly appear to,' I said. 'Although I have to admit to being a bit confused about the whole thing. How did you even *know* a guy like Dougie Dowds? It's hard to imagine the two of you moving in the same social circles.'

Brian shut his eyes. 'I didn't know him,' he said. 'He just turned up at the door one night about a month ago, and told me he'd some information concerning Wilma's future happiness that I might be interested in.'

'He was looking for a bung?'

Brian nodded. 'He asked me for a hundred quid, then told me he'd heard Vince had stolen a valuable painting, in case I wanted to warn Wilma about what she might be getting herself into. I was glad to pay him. I appreciated the service. But at the time, Wilma seemed to be happy for the first time in years – truly happy – and I didn't want to destroy that. So I decided later not to tell her. And I thought, chances are, Vince might never get caught anyway.'

'I daresay your keenness to get your hands on that cancelled alimony played a part in your decision as well,' I said, but he just narrowed his eyes at me, suggesting the way I thought was beneath contempt, and he battered on, telling me how Dougie had phoned up a couple of weeks later and asked how Wilma had taken the news.

'I told him I'd decided to keep the information to myself,' he said. 'And then he told me he'd been offered a deal by the police – immunity for a crime he'd committed in exchange for the same piece of information he'd given me, and that he was going to take the deal. I asked him to reconsider, knowing it would mean the end of Wilma's happiness if Vince got arrested. He said there was nothing he could do, and I asked him to at least hold off until I'd talked to him in person. So I went round . . . and the rest you know.'

I suppose, when you look at it in a certain light, it's quite a romantic story really – an ex-husband dedicated to the future happiness of his ex-wife. As long as you can manage to ignore the loss of a human life, that is.

'Anyway,' Brian said, rallying again after his earlier mini-breakdown, 'it's all water under the bridge now. What's done is done. And I've got a more immediate crisis on my hands now, after slipping up and confessing the whole shambles to you.'

He bent forwards and checked the integrity of my constraints, then he scratched his head. 'Mind you,' he said, 'I daresay you've got a better idea of what I should do next than I have. What kind of thing would you do in a situation like this?'

'Eh?'

'Methods,' he said. 'I suppose I'm looking for a bit of advice. How would *you* . . . eliminate . . . somebody like you in a situation like this.'

I could hardly believe my ears.

'*You're* the fucking murderer, pal,' I said. 'What in the name of Christ are you talking about? You're the one that's fresh from killing wee Dougie Dowds. You're just after admitting that.'

'Aye,' he said, 'but that was an accident. I've already told you. This is the first time I've ever had to kill somebody deliberately. I'm an architect, for God's sake. *You're* the criminal. You're the one with the expertise in this field.'

I was really starting to believe that this whole thing might actually be a dream. A right corker of a dream, granted, but a dream all the same. Then I came to the conclusion that even *my* formidable unconscious mind could never come up with something on this scale. Plus, the outrageous pain caused by the ovenware served to assure me that the whole thing was real.

'Tell me this, Brian,' I said, 'have you ever read any books by Ian Rankin – the Rebus stuff?'

He thought about it for a minute. 'Now that you mention it, I think I've read one or two. A while ago.'

'How about one called *A Question of Blood*?' I said. 'The one with me in it? Have you read that? Cause I think you're maybe labouring under a false impression of who I actually am, pal. In real life, I've never been done for so much as light GBH, Brian, never mind *killed* a guy. I'm an ideas man, with a part-time sideline in petty theft to pay the bills. *You're* the one that should be in a fucking Rankin book, instead of hiding behind this "I'm an architect" bullshit. I've got news for you, pal. You're no longer an architect – you're a fucking murderer and you'd better fucking get used to it.'

But my rant appeared to have been lost on him. He was off in a wee world of his own, pontificating. And then he came to, with a bright smile on his face, looking as pleased as punch.

'I think you might be on to something,' he said, and wandered off and started opening and closing drawers, looking for God knows what. 'I hadn't thought of that. Ian Rankin, that's a good idea. I'm glad I read those books now. Never really enjoyed them at the time, but there was a wheen of stuff in there I could use for guidance.'

'That's not what I was meaning.'

'Either way, I think you're on to something. Ah, here we are now.'

Now, personally I don't spend all that much time in the kitchen. I can put a passable fry-up together, heat up a tin of soup and what have you, but I'm not particularly au fait with the correct terms and uses for the barrage of utensils you'd find strewn about the average kitchen. Nevertheless, I feel pretty confident in stating that what Brian had pulled from the drawer, and found very much to his liking, was a dirty great meat cleaver. The blade was almost square, a beast of a thing, and the edge looked as sharp as a razor blade.

'Now wait a minute there . . .' I said as he came stoating across the room towards me, brandishing it proudly. He might very well have been telling the truth when he claimed that hurling Dougie Dowds over that balcony rail had been entirely accidental, but now that he'd stumbled upon a new vocation he seemed determined to dedicate himself to it with gusto. It was hard to ignore the fact that what he'd most likely done was discover his true calling on the twenty-third of June, after a barrage of wasted years mistakenly thinking he'd been put on God's green earth to design low-cost housing and multi-storey car parks.

'Easy does it,' he said as he dropped down to his knees

in front of me and moved the butcher's blade about in a worrying manner. 'If you try anything funny here, I'll have your leg off at the knee. All right?'

Then he ran the cleaver down through the tape that was securing my left ankle to the leg of the chair and pulled my foot midway between the two chair legs. He looked up at me for my response and I nodded, then he did the same thing to the tape round my right leg and pulled that in towards the other one.

He'd the roll of duct tape down there on the floor beside him, and as he ripped off a strip I considered my chances of kicking him quickly in the face before he'd time to lash out at me with his weapon. It was no doubt doable, but the odds of me getting enough force into it to be certain I'd avoid a chibbing seemed low, especially when you took into account the size of the guy and the fact that I'd still be strapped to the chair afterwards, with my hands tied behind my back. So I sat there like a tadger while he taped my ankles together, then he stood up and jabbed the cleaver at the left-hand side of my chest, cutting the tape that was there, and going round to the other side to do the same.

'Right,' he said then. 'That's you. Stand up.'

I frowned at him. 'What for?'

'Cause we're going for a drive,' he said. 'You were spot on with that Ian Rankin idea. Cheers for that. Stand up!'

He punctuated the suggestion by pushing the front edge

of the knife against my arm, which was actually quite persuasive, so I gave it a go.

I'm sure you know what it's like trying to raise yourself from a sitting position with your ankles bound together and your arms tied behind your back. Not easy. Especially when your sense of balance has been adversely affected by a severe blow to the head. But I got there. I got there, and then I wondered what next – my options seemed somewhat limited.

'The garage is just through that door there,' Brian said. 'Let's go. Nice and easy.'

'What the fuck are you talking about?' I asked him. 'Look at me! I can't fucking move. Are you taking the piss, Brian?'

'Bounce,' he told me. 'Just jump. Come on.'

'Cut the tape,' I told him. 'I'll walk there. Stop acting like a prick.'

'I can't risk it,' he said. 'I don't trust you.' He turned the sharp end of the blade towards me and laid it against my chest. 'Start bouncing,' he said. 'Now!'

So I gave it a shot, and like I'd imagined, it was a non-starter. I got about three feet and then I couped backwards. And I landed on the kitchen floor with a bang. I felt as if I'd burst my fucking lungs.

'For Christ's sake,' Brian said, standing over me.

I lay there looking up at him. 'What the fuck were you expecting?' I said.

He shook his head. 'Don't move,' he said. 'I've got an idea. Give me a minute. You're a fucking liability, Peacock.'

And then it was just me lying there. Wondering exactly what he had in mind. And wishing I'd gone straight to Stewart Street when I'd had the chance, rather than taking John Jack's daft advice and coming here first.

13

It's funny the things that go through your mind when you're lying trussed up in the boot of a BMW, being driven at speed to what you can only assume will be your final resting place. I'm sure you've had a similar experience yourself at some point, and that you've found yourself focusing on your biggest regrets in life, the things you wished you'd done but that you never quite got round to. That's what was going on in my case anyway, and what I found myself honing in on was the idea that if I could have my time again, I'd have done a bit more reading. I'd have used my days a bit more wisely in that regard.

Now – don't get me wrong – it's not the highbrow stuff I would've gone for. I was untroubled regarding my ignorance of Shakespeare or Wordsworth, Dostoevsky or Stephen King. I was quite content to go to my grave never having suffered the indignity of trudging my way through any of that mince. But if I could have gone back in time by even a month or two, what I would have done was applied myself assiduously to the works of the boy Rankin. That's where I felt I'd made my greatest mistake. If I'd ploughed through his back catalogue when I'd had the chance, I'd no doubt have been able to work out what plotline Brian was in the process of plagiarising – and could have come up with a plan to get myself out of it in some way.

As things stood, though, I'd only ever read the book Rankin had papped me in, and even getting through that one had been a bit of a chore. It was somewhat light on the joie de vivre, if you know what I mean. So I couldn't even begin to fathom what Brian's plans might be, which put me at a distinct disadvantage when it came to thinking of a way of trying to counteract them.

I'd had one brainwave back at his abode while the two of us were struggling to fold me up into the boot, hampered somewhat in our efforts by my inability to do much manoeuvring myself and Brian's general sense of impatience at getting me in there.

The idea had struck me while he was dragging me across the kitchen floor on a blanket he'd encouraged me to roll on to, and I'd felt certain I'd come up with a robust plan that was fully capable of doing the business.

'Are you sure all this fucking about is absolutely necessary, Brian?' I'd said, when he had me standing up in the internal garage and he was unlocking the boot of the car.

'I wish it wasn't,' he said. 'We've always been good

pals, Peacock, but you can see the fix I'm in. This is the only solution.'

'Maybe there's another one, though,' I said. 'You know what I'm like, eh? I'm an ideas man, Brian. All that matters to me are my ideas. Everything else is purely secondary. Background noise.'

He pushed down on my shoulders, forcing me to sit on the edge of the boot, then he bent down and lifted my feet. 'Lean back and spin round,' he said, and he pushed my feet, bending me further at the knees.

I did what he told me and crowned myself on the underside of the boot lid.

'This fingerprint idea means everything to me, Brian,' I said. 'Seriously. And your private life's your own affair, as far as I'm concerned. As long as you're still willing to invest in my future, that's good enough for me. Your financial backing buys my silence, permanently. Why the fuck would I want to see you in jail when it would mean the end of my business?'

He gave it some welly with the pushing, and I wriggled about this way and that, and finally I was lying flat on my back in the boot of the car, looking up at him imploringly.

For a minute it even seemed like he might be buying it, then the possibility passed. 'It's too big a risk,' he said.

'How?' I asked him. 'Where's the risk? If I ever breathed a word of it to anybody, my funding would be gone. The business would go tits up. It's airtight, Brian – rock solid.'

He shook his head. 'The business might succeed,' he said, 'in a big way. Then you'd be financially secure, and the day might come when we'd have a disagreement about something.'

He ripped a generous strip off the roll of duct tape and slapped it across my gub, putting paid to any further communication on my part. I'd been wanting to ask him, if all else failed, just exactly what it was he had in mind for me, where it was we were going, but even that was out of the question now.

He started battering tape across my body, pinning me to the floor of the boot, and attaching my feet so I couldn't lift them either. It struck me as overkill, but it seemed to keep him happy. And once he'd given it all a good hard tug to make sure it was nice and solid, he stood looking down at me and gave me a friendly wee nod. Then he reached up for the boot lid and thumped it shut authoritatively.

And I was in total darkness.

From the time the car started moving, as well as being consumed by regrets about my reading habits, I was also following every turn we made and estimating how far we travelled between each turn, trying to work out exactly where we were going. I knew for certain we'd turned left at the end of Brian's driveway, and then right when we'd reached the main road, but everything after that had the air of speculation about it. I felt pretty certain we'd gone into the centre of town, and from there headed for the Expressway, but I was well aware I could easily have made some fundamental error along the way, and the truth of the matter might be that we were in a totally different part of the city from the one I was picturing.

Nevertheless, the fact that I was strapped up like Houdini, and the general direction I imagined we were travelling in, made it seem odds-on favourite that what Brian was planning to do was dump me in the Clyde, in a state that would make swimming something of a non-starter.

I imagined them fishing my body out of the Firth in a couple of weeks' time, bloated beyond all recognition, so that they'd have to identify me by the state of my teeth. Then some genius at police headquarters would conclude that it had been bound to come to me sooner or later, if what he'd read about my gun-running and drug-dealing in Rankin's book was anything to go by. The police would no doubt make one or two idle inquiries here and there and draw a blank, concluding that this kind of thing happens all the time amongst gangsters – nothing really for them to get involved in – and Brian would be off scot-free. Utterly unsuspected. McFadgen would be delighted I was off the streets, the mother-in-law would start trying to coax the wife out onto the dating scene at the earliest possible opportunity, and it would probably only be Bev herself who would be in any way bothered I was gone.

Then I had a happier thought. It occurred to me that if this scenario *was* something Brian had ripped off from a Rankin novel, it was very unlikely the killer in that book had used something as pishy as duct tape to tie his victim up before plunging them into the cold dark depths. More likely it had been rope, or chains. There was a right good chance, in my opinion, that duct tape might fail to keep its consistency in water – especially water as chemically toxic as the Clyde. The stuff was bound to expand, weaken – *melt* even. As long as I could keep myself afloat long enough maybe I'd make it. Brian was a rank amateur, I had that on my side. I'd no doubt catch some pretty manky disease from the river, but I'd recover from that – in time. Maybe things weren't quite as bleak as I'd been painting them after all.

The car stopped. If this was our final destination, my calculations were way off. I was aware of the driver's door opening, and slamming shut again, then the soft thud of the central-locking system sparking up. That, in itself, was unexpected. If he was coming to get me out of the boot, what the fuck was he locking it for? He must be having a scout around first, making sure nobody else was about – wherever the hell we were.

Then a second possibility occurred to me: maybe this was just a quick stop-off on the way to our journey's end. My navigating had been good enough, and he was just nipping into a shop for something he'd need as part of his plan. My heart sank at that, cause it meant he'd more than likely had the same insight I'd had myself – that the tape would loosen up in the water. He was no doubt off on a jaunt to acquire some rope, or even just something nice and heavy he could attach me to, to make sure I went down like a bad joke and didn't come back up again.

I tried wriggling about. If we were in the vicinity of a shop there might be some folk about, and if I could manage to bash at the underside of the boot maybe one of them would hear me. I pushed myself one way and then the other. Nothing. He'd fixed me in good and proper. I tried pushing my tongue against the strip of tape across my mouth, but there was nothing doing there, either. A couple of go's and the gag reflex kicked in, which definitely didn't seem desirable, given the chances of me choking to death on my own vomit.

I calmed my beans. 'Patience, Peacock,' I told myself. 'Patience, son. Save your energy for when you'll need it.'

Here's the thing, though – I'm pretty sure a good hour must have passed without there being any sign of Brian returning to the scene of the crime. It's probably even harder to estimate how long you've spent lying in a darkened boot than it is to try and follow where you're being taken when you can't see the road, especially when a quick glance at your watch is totally out of the question. But it certainly felt like a hell of a long time. And then I started to think that maybe this was just it. Maybe at some point he'd come back and slip a hose into the boot and attach it to the exhaust, and leave the car running till I was done. Or maybe he just wouldn't *come* back. Maybe I'd just be lying here till I croaked from lack of water, and that would be it. How long does that take? Forty-eight hours? Something like that?

I think I started to have a panic attack then. Maybe dehydration wasn't even necessary. Maybe he knew the boot was airtight enough that I'd soon have used up all the oxygen, and then I'd just peg out. I could feel it happening. My head was light, each breath seemed harder and harder to take. My life started flashing before my eyes.

And the worst of it was, it wasn't even my *whole* life that was doing the flashing – it was really just a concentrated chunk of it, the past week or so, in every excruciatingly arsed-up detail. My excitement about getting the fingerprint business off the ground. McFadgen crashing in on my plans with his mad theory that I'd whacked Dougie Dowds. My idiot idea of finding out from John Jack who was really responsible for stealing the painting. My bampot attempt to keep McFadgen from finding out it was Vince Cowie that had taken it. My moronic decision to go and fill Brian in on what was happening rather than going straight to Stewart Street and getting myself locked up there and then. I could be sitting pretty in a cell right now, instead of lying in here replaying all of this shite against my will, slowly suffocating – or waiting to be drowned –

or waiting for a pipe to slide in through the back seat and start pumping carbon monoxide into my lungs.

Then the panic attack passed, and I was back to just lying there again. And if I'm being perfectly honest, although I should have been savouring each precious moment I had left on this earth, I actually started to feel quite bored. I was certain another hour had passed, and then another one. And finally, when I'd probably drifted off to sleep, I heard a thump like a hand battering down on the lid of the boot, then the unmistakable clatter of the central-locking system springing into action. Then a click, then a creak, and the cold rush of air flooding into the car as the boot finally opened.

It turned out, though, when I looked up towards Brian, that I had yet another disaster on my plate. Maybe, I thought, this is a further symptom of the severe blow to the head, or maybe I popped something vital during my panic attack – but whatever the cause was, there was no getting away from the fact that I now appeared to be blind.

Totally sightless.

I could hear the dickhead breathing, and I could hear his feet shuffling about on the road, but, visually, complete blackness was the order of the day.

I blinked hard, scrunched my face up – nothing. I tried again, and this time when I opened my eyes, it was the opposite problem, an extreme experience of explosive light. Then I got a handle on what was actually happening. I wasn't blind at all. I'd spent so long lying in the boot of the car that it was nighttime – pitch dark outside – and now the donkey was shining a torch into the boot. As he moved it away from my face, it gave my eyes a chance to adjust and I could see his outline against the sky, and gradually – in the reflected light from the torch – I was able to actually see his face.

Something weird had happened to it. His cheeks seemed swollen, and his teeth looked all fucked up. And then, as my eyes continued to improve, I worked out what had happened. This wasn't actually Brian I was staring at. I'd been mistaken. It was somebody else altogether. Are you ready for this? No word of a lie, I was actually staring straight up into the knackered face of the omnipresent officer of the law, the brave Detective Inspector Duncan McFadgen.

Police clown extraordinaire.

'I knew from the off you were mixed up in this, Johnson,' he said. Then he took a step back, still shining his torch on my taped-up body, and one of the goons who had been shadowing him when I met him in that manky café stepped forwards into the light. He was carrying a knife, and he started prodding about amongst the tape that was holding me pinned to the floor of the boot. Then he noticed the bit of tape across my face and reached up to whip it off.

'Leave that,' McFadgen said, and grabbed the lackey's arm before he could do any damage. 'We don't need to be listening to any of his shite on the drive back to the station. Just cut him out of there and leave it at that.'

So the minion did what he was told. He freed my feet, but left my hands trussed up behind my back, and he spun me into a sitting position with my legs dangling out over the edge.

'Take a minute to get the blood flowing again,' he said, then McFadgen took hold of my arm and they marched me towards a police car that was sitting behind the BMW.

I was at a total loss as to what the fuck was going on. McFadgen eased me into the back seat with a hand on top of my head, for all the world as if my wrists were in handcuffs. The minion got into the driver's seat, McFadgen flopped into the passenger side, and then we were off.

I tried puffing my cheeks up in the hope that it would dislodge the tape, so I could ask them what in the name of Christ had led to this unexpected turn of events, but the tape wouldn't budge, and it hurt like fuck.

'If I'd thought I could get away with it, I'd have left him in there,' McFadgen said to the lackey. 'Trust me. You've no idea the bullshit we're in for when we remove that muzzle. I should have got an order from above to carry out a controlled explosion on the vehicle. Told the boss I'd reason to believe the perpetrator put a bomb in the boot.'

I made as loud a noise as I could – just to register my disapproval – then I looked out the side widow and ignored his yammering for the rest of the journey.

And I hoped to fuck I wasn't on my way to finding out that this prick had just saved my fucking life.

14

I don't know if Wilma Caldwell had been expecting her wedding day to be one of the best days of her life. When you've already been through it once before, you pretty much know the drill, and you no doubt adjust your outlook to be more in keeping with reality. So like I say, I don't know what Wilma's expectations were, leading up to the thing. But I *do* know that for the past couple of months I'd been expecting her wedding to be one of the best days of *my* life. I'd been building it up as the moment a new future would open up before me, full of possibility and hope for a better time to come, a day full of joy and wonder and celebration. And yet, here I was, all of that having gone right up the spout, simply stuck at yet another run-of-the-mill wedding, with all the tedium and repetition that entails.

Fucking brutal.

'Look at the face on Shirley Miller,' the wife was saying. 'Sitting up there at the head table like she's the Queen of

Sheba. Unbelievable. Let *me* tell *you*, Peacock, she is *not* the Queen of Sheba – far from it. And I should know. Whatever possessed Wilma to pick her as the maid of honour, I'll never know. Wilma's only known her for about ten minutes, if that. How long have I known Wilma for, Peacock? Eh? How come I'm not sitting up there? How come I'm just a normal bridesmaid? Tell me that.'

'I thought you said you didn't want anybody looking at you in your dress,' I said. 'If you were sitting up there you'd be the centre of attention. Bang slap in the middle of everybody's wedding pictures.'

'True,' she said. 'But still, it's the principle of the thing. It should be me that's the maid of honour. And they'll be getting their meals first – and theirs'll be much bigger than ours.'

'They'll be just the same.'

'But they'll get them first. And I'm starving. What was it Wilma said we're getting again? Can you remember? Was it salmon? I hope it's not salmon. I don't really like salmon. Why is it everybody always has salmon at the minute? I think salmon maybe brings me out in a rash.'

Another couple came and plonked themselves down at our table, and that quietened her down for a bit. Christ knows who they were. Craig and Wendy their place names said. They looked like a right couple of warmers. I started wishing Brian had taken the liberty of tipping me into the river while he'd had the chance.

'Are you Craig and Wendy?' the wife said. 'I saw your names sitting there. We're Bev and Peacock. It's been a lovely day, hasn't it? So far.'

Craig and Wendy gave it the strained smiles, and Wendy even went so far as to say it was nice to meet us.

'What did you think of the ceremony?' Bev said. 'It was gorgeous, wasn't it? I promised myself I wouldn't start greeting. Fat chance. Once I got started I thought I'd never stop. Did you see me? I made a right fool of myself. I'm terrible, amn't I, Peacock? I just hope the speeches don't get too emotional, or I'll be off again.'

As it turned out, in that particular instance, she got her wish – especially where the father-of-the-bride's speech was concerned. I mean, it started off conventionally enough. He stood up – in a dark blue suit that was a couple of sizes too big for him, his wispy grey hair squashed down with Brylcreem, the collar of his shirt too wide for his neck – and he ran through a few well-rehearsed jokes, as old as the hills, and a set-piece about how he wasn't so much gaining a new son-in-law as losing the social stigma that came with having a middle-aged divorcee for a daughter.

All very middle-of-the-road and par for the course. But then, about five minutes in, he veered off spectacularly into uncharted territory, fuelled by an abundance of sherry and the sheer madness of the events of the past week or so, and he was soon miles off script and improvising a rather unique and entertaining piece of oratory.

'Let's just hope,' he said, taking another large swig from his glass and beginning to slur his words quite liberally, 'let's just hope Vince turns out to be a slightly less *interesting* husband than the maniac Wilma married the first time around. Not that Brian ever seemed particularly interesting in all the time Wilma was with him, mind. I vividly recall many a tedious evening spent in the man's company, during his years as a law-abiding citizen. But I think we can all agree that these past few days have revealed a side to the man that's a great deal more colourful than any of us had previously given him credit for. And I now find myself in the unlikely position of admitting that as long as Vince can refrain from getting himself chased halfway across the continent by Europol, then he'll be a marked improvement on my previous son-in-law.'

It was a good point: the bar was now quite low regarding what Vince would have to live up to in order to look like a good catch. Whether he'd manage to pull it off, though, was another matter. There was every chance he'd be on the run soon enough himself, or sitting in a prison cell wishing he'd gone on the run.

'I'm reliably informed,' Wilma's old man continued, 'that my ex-son-in-law is currently somewhere between Frankfurt and Munich, suspected to be heading for the Austrian border, and leading the authorities on a merry dance, having now attained the status of being the most wanted man in Western Europe.'

That last quip was a bit of an exaggeration – no doubt added in to enhance the drama – but it certainly had its basis in fact. Brian had even made it on to the STV news that morning – a man from Glasgow at large somewhere on the continent, guilty of having left an innocent victim bound and gagged in the boot of a car for upwards of five hours, and suspected of having murdered a local criminal by the name of Dougie Dowds. Police said it was likely that drugs were involved. Thankfully, word hadn't got out that I was the stooge in the boot – not to the public at large anyway. I'd asked McFadgen to do me the favour of keeping that quiet for the time being, in exchange for the information I was in a position to give him about the Brian fellow.

At this point, the bride's mother more or less rugby-tackled her husband to get him off the microphone, and we returned to more mainstream wedding territory again – the best man, a right bore of hell, giving it laldy about Vince's early sexual experiences and various minor mis-demeanours, and then the groom himself, essentially just thanking the cast and crew for a good hour and a quarter.

When it all finally clattered to a halt, and much to the wife's relief they started to serve the grub, I felt a light tap on my shoulder and turned round to see Vince was standing there beside my chair.

'Congratulations,' our tablemate Craig told him, and Wendy had a good go at insisting how enjoyable the speeches had been, but Vince himself was somewhat distracted.

'Can we have a quick word, Peacock?' he said, looking to the right and the left at regular intervals. 'Somewhere quiet?'

And off we went, leaving the wife to start firing into her crab cakes, as content as could be.

When McFadgen had bundled me into an interrogation room and sat himself down on the other side of the table, I was still fully taped up, and still wearing the strip across my piehole.

'Right,' he'd said, 'you're about to explain to me exactly what's going on here, after I fill you in on the full extent of my knowledge at the present time.'

There were only the two of us in there, and McFadgen claimed that about an hour ago they'd had an anonymous phone call at the station saying there was somebody locked in the boot of a car down by the Clyde, just beyond the Transport Museum, and that the car key was under a rock beside the front passenger wheel.

'I was all set to clock off,' McFadgen said. 'Thirty-six hours straight I've just done. Then I hear about this phone call on my way out the door. It turns out the officer that took it had the wherewithal to ask the caller if he could supply the identity of the individual in the boot, and after a protracted silence the caller gave her your name and hung up. Naturally I got excited. "Did the caller say if it was a dead body?" I asked her. He hadn't specified. As you've probably noticed, I'm still trying to shake the disappointment of finding out you were still breathing in there.'

All heart, eh? You've got to hand it to McFadgen. Six hours it turns out I'd spent in that confined space, constantly awaiting my execution, and that was as much sympathy as McFadgen could muster. Now, whether Brian had always intended to just lock me up in the boot of the BMW to keep me quiet long enough for him to make his getaway, or whether he'd initially been planning to kill me and then bottled it and come up with his harebrained scheme on the fly, I've still no idea. But I'd certainly been under the impression that my number was up during my confinement, and a smidgeon of compassion from the man of the law wouldn't have gone amiss at that point in time. It would have been very much welcome. But it was far from forthcoming.

He got to his feet. 'I'm about to remove that gag now,' he said. 'But I don't want any shite out of you. Cold hard facts, nothing less: who phoned us, why, what this is all about. That's it. I want this done and dusted so I can get home to my bed.'

And he yanked at the tape with relish, enjoying it tearing chunks of the moustache out at the root.

It hurt like a bastard.

Poor Vince Cowie wasn't looking too clever as we stoated about the venue, trying to find a quiet alcove for our confab. The boy was a nervous wreck, and it clearly wasn't just a case of the wedding-day jitters. Whenever a guest approached him to express their congratulations, each time we thought we'd found a spot that would suffice, he'd look like a startled rabbit, and we'd be off again seeking ever deeper seclusion. I got the distinct impression that he was on the verge of a psychotic episode.

Eventually we found ourselves outside the establishment entirely, standing behind a monumental oak tree on the lawns that sloped down from the place. After Vince had walked round the trunk of the thing six or seven times he seemed to be satisfied, and he sat down with his back against it and stared up at the branches.

'So what's the story?' he asked me then, and I moved round so I was standing in front of him. There was no way in hell I was flopping down on the floor myself, risking getting grass stains on the Versaces. Not a chance.

'Eh?' I said. I'd no idea what he was getting at, as sympathetic as I was to his obvious state of anguish.

'Am I fucked?' he said. 'I know it was you that worked out Brian killed Dougie Dowds, and told the filth about it. I'd no idea Brian was capable of something like that, but you must know I was involved at the business end – taking that painting. Am I knackered? Did you fill them in on that?'

A big crow landed in the branches above him, and he just about shat himself before he sussed where the noise had come from.

'I think you've got your wires crossed, Vince,' I said. 'It wasn't so much a case of me going to the authorities as it was of Brian delivering me to them himself.'

I unfurled the whole scenario for him – meat cleaver included – and he took it all in, in wide-eyed wonder, and expressed his deepest sympathies come the end.

'Fucking hell, Peacock!' he said. 'That's fucking mental.'

'You're not wrong, son,' I told him. 'But you can rest easy for the time being. I kept your name completely out of my report to McFadgen. I've been trying to keep him off your tail for a good while now. I've known you took that painting for yonks, but I wanted to play my part in making sure the old wedding came to fruition. I told McFadgen it must have been Brian that stole the painting. Stands to reason.'

And luckily for Vince, Jinky hadn't even known that a painting had been stolen from Pollok House. Despite all my worries, Jinky could have stayed in the interrogation room for a month, and McFadgen would still have been no closer to the truth.

Vince looked genuinely moved on hearing what I'd done for him. He even got up off his arse and gave me a wee dunt on the upper arm.

'You're some man,' he said. 'I'm serious. I owe you big time, Peacock. So what did McFadgen make of the whole thing? Was he buying the idea that Brian stole the painting?'

I shrugged. 'Fuck knows,' I said. 'I'd a hell of a job even convincing him the horror show with Brian actually happened. "How do I know Brian Caldwell's not just away on his holidays?" he said. Something like that. "There's a good chance you just stuck yourself in the boot of his car and cooked this whole thing up to take the heat off yourself." The prick's obsessed with putting me in Barlinnie. "What about the fact that Brian phoned you?" I asked him. "That could've been anybody," he said. "How in the name of Christ would I have managed to tape myself into the boot of the car and leave the key outside?" "Obviously you'd a pal involved." McFadgen's far from being the brightest star in the sky, Vince. He's unlikely to work out you'd anything to do with it before they get their hands on Brian. Once that happens, it all comes down to whether Brian decides to put you in the shit, or just keep schtum.'

A huge burden seemed to lift from his shoulders. His eyes lit up. He suddenly looked like what he was – a man who had just married the latest love of his life.

'That's good enough for me,' he said. 'We're honeymooning in Spain. I don't think it'll be too much of a stretch to convince Wilma to take a prolonged trip down on the Costa del Sol. Then we can take it one day at a time. I know a few folk down there who'll no doubt hook me up with something or other.'

'That sounds like a plan,' I said. 'Kick back in the sunshine. Live it up.'

He dusted the arse of his pants and then said he'd better

be getting back to the festivities. 'Come on up and we'll get some Champagne,' he said, but I told him to go on ahead.

'I'll get a wee bit more of this fresh air and then I'll see you up there,' I said.

'You're sure?'

'Positive. It's a nice spot out here, I'll stay and soak it up for a bit. I'll see you in there.'

I stood and watched him skipping up the lawn, back towards the celebrations, and then I turned about and took in the scenery. There was a good reason I'd decided to stay on for a bit, over and above the conversational carnage that awaited me inside at the dinner table. And it was this: while the two of us had been standing there, idly chewing the fat, it had gradually come to my attention that, besides our voices and the sound of the odd bird here and there, the place was awash with silence. We must have been miles away from a main road, nowhere near a flight path, and with everybody else tucked away behind the thick stone walls of the old country house at the top of the lawn, the conditions were absolutely perfect for an ideas man in need of a new idea. And if there was one thing I was in need of at this particular point in history, it was definitely a new idea.

Brian Caldwell had been the only person on the planet prepared to put his weight behind the fingerprint thing, and that ship had well and truly sailed. Reflecting on it now, that was probably for the best. Judging by his recent behaviour, I wasn't entirely convinced he actually had the kind of temperament I'd be looking for in a long-term business partner.

I walked further down the hill, towards a path that led off into a wheen of trees and greenery, and I just let the silence soak into the depths of me. Maybe John Jack had been right – maybe DNA was the thing nowadays, maybe my idea as it stood would have had limited appeal. I severely doubted it, but I decided it was best, under the current circumstances, to at least allow that as a possibility, in the hope it would be easier to move on.

At the bottom of the hill I turned around and looked up at the venue again, realising that it was pretty much down to me that this celebration was going ahead. If I hadn't been wanting to keep McFadgen away from Vince, and just wanted McFadgen off my back, Vince would no doubt be in the slammer right now, with this whole match abandoned. A fat lot of good it had done me, though. I'd gotten hee-haw out of it – absolutely zilch, except this silence. This wee minute of quiet.

But maybe that would be enough. Maybe everything else had just been a preliminary to get me here, into position to receive the big one, the game changer, the idea that would catapult me from the day-to-day grind of nicking and scheming, out into the pale blue yonder, out into the world of luxury and ease, out into the sunshine and sand, the wife stoating along beside me with a great big smile on her face, nattering about this, that and the next thing as we tried to decide which upmarket resort to winter in this year, and whether we should go for the Picasso or the Rubens for the front room.

I walked longways across the lawns. It was bound to come, my idea. It was a rare thing indeed to come across a peace and quiet like this, and it was probably only the noise and chatter of everyday life that had prevented me from connecting with the monster that I knew must be waiting in the back bit of my brain. So I walked, and I listened, and I waited. 'Patience, son,' I said. 'Patience, Peacock.'

There was no doubt at all that that was what was needed. That was the only thing that was presently required.